**THE PATHS OF S**

She had arranged to arrive at ten o'clock, and
was only a few minutes late as she knocked
at the door, feeling as though her legs were
made of sawdust. Mike himself opened it.
In navy blue roll-top sweater, navy trousers
and canvas shoes, he had changed from
lawyer to Cornishman. She could read nothing
from his expression. It was as stony as
Brighton beach.
'I've nothing to say to you and can't imagine
why you've come. I'll give you fifteen minutes,
Josephine, to say what you want to say,
and then go.'

It was only the recollection of the old Mike
that kept her from walking out on this arrogant,
unyielding stranger. She drew a deep breath
and said quietly,

'I want to tell you what happened. . .'

# The Paths
# of Summer

---

# Iris Bromige

CORONET BOOKS
Hodder and Stoughton

Copyright © 1979 by Iris Bromige

First published in Great Britain 1979 by
Hodder and Stoughton Limited

*Coronet edition 1981*


**British Library C.I.P.**

Bromige, Iris
    The paths of summer.
    I. Title
    823'.914[F]        PR6052.R572

ISBN 0–340–26098–X

Printed and bound in Great Britain for
Hodder and Stoughton Paperbacks, a
division of Hodder and Stoughton Ltd.,
Mill Road, Dunton Green, Sevenoaks,
Kent (Editorial Office : 47 Bedford
Square, London, WC1 3DP) by
Richard Clay (The Chaucer Press) Ltd,
Bungay, Suffolk

# Contents

# 1

# A Touch of Spring

Conrad Ravensburg finished dictating and leaned back in his chair with a satisfied smile.

"That should ruffle a few feathers," he observed to the young woman on the other side of the desk. "If you can't improve on it, Josephine, send it off to the editor with my compliments."

And if, thought Josephine, anybody had the temerity to claim to be able to improve the writing of that eminent man of letters, Conrad Ravensburg, the benign expression on the handsome face of her employer would be replaced by a very frosty one indeed. But, discreetly, she edited a good deal of his journalistic work these days.

"That request to speak at the Dilford Literary Society meeting in May. Have you decided?"

"I think we'll turn that one down, my dear. Pressure of work, and all that. Sincere regrets with all your usual tact and charm." His eyes rested on her with approval as he added, "What should I do without you, Josephine? How did I ever manage before a blessed providence dropped you in my path?"

"Very well, I'm sure," said Josephine, smiling.

"Well, I shall never cease to bless the editor of that, alas now defunct, local paper that sent you to interview me. And a very good job you made of it, I remember. For a young girl of twenty, a remarkably able piece of journalism."

"I thought I'd arrived, being sent to interview the

famous Conrad Ravensburg, and I was more than a little nervous."

"It didn't show. I recognised your potential immediately, and gained an invaluable recruit. I flatter myself that my training and guidance have brought you on, but the potential was always there. Wasted on that obscure little paper, and, if I may say so, on that farouche young man you were engaged to."

"That all seems a long time ago."

"Yes, indeed. You've travelled a long way since then, my dear. Which reminds me that it's time I raised your salary. As my personal assistant, you're worth more than money can buy, but one shouldn't lose sight of practicalities."

"I'm more than generously paid."

He waved a hand.

"I shall give it some thought. Ever heard from that young man? Brentwood?"

"Wexford. Michael Wexford. No, I haven't heard anything from him."

She looked at her employer thoughtfully, wondering why he had brought Mike's name up after all these years. Experience had taught her that his remarks were seldom aimless. He met her look with a bland expression. Now in his late sixties, his light blue eyes were unusually bright and keen for a man of his years. With aquiline features, immaculately groomed silver hair and a pink complexion, allied to a tall slender figure, he was still a man of great charm and attraction. She had been bowled over by him at that first youthful encounter and although experience had tempered her first unquestioning hero-worship, she still felt the potency of his charm, while her admiration for his exceptional talent with words had only increased over the years.

"No regrets, I'm sure. You were a child then. It would have been tragic to have been snatched up by that young man and buried in domesticity. I only mention it because I thought I saw him, or someone like him, driving out of the car park in Dilford yesterday. Probably mistaken. I only saw him once or twice, after all. Now, what time am I supposed to be opening this library extension tomorrow?"

She gave him the details and went to her office to start on the day's correspondence. While it would be untrue to say that she had never given Michael Wexford a thought during these past four busy and exciting years, indeed for the first months after the breaking of their engagement she had been haunted by him, for the past year and more he had become a pale ghost, troubling her very little. Now, as she inserted the paper in her typewriter, she dismissed her employer's reminder of that distant, shadowy past, and concentrated on her work, for she had a busy day in front of her.

She was still working on the proofs of Conrad's latest biography when he came into her office soon after five o'clock, looking devastatingly handsome in evening dress, for he was due at a dinner in London that night.

"Is your car still in dock, my dear?" he asked.

"Yes. It won't be ready until Friday."

"Then let John drop you off on our way. Time you stopped work."

"Thank you, but I'd like to finish checking this chapter, and it's a nice evening for the walk home. I shall quite enjoy it."

"As you wish, my dear." He sniffed the white carnation in his buttonhole. "Trust the food and wine will be rather more inspiring this evening than they were when I last attended a dinner at this hotel. The company, then, I seem to remember, was exceedingly dreary, too."

"Well, your speech will enliven things tonight."

"It is rather a good one, don't you think?"

"Very stimulating."

"All the same, with a two hour drive up to London, through numerous traffic jams, no doubt, and not home until the small hours, I wonder if it's worth it."

"Why do you accept so many invitations?" asked Josephine with a demure voice and a twinkle in her eyes, for she knew that Conrad loved being fêted at social gatherings.

"Well," he said expansively, waving a hand, "one has a position to uphold on the literary scene, and a duty to one's profession. We have several quite eminent guests from abroad to welcome this evening. Should be an interesting occasion."

She stood at the window and watched the silver grey Rolls Royce move silently down the drive. Conrad certainly upheld his position, she thought, half smiling as she turned back to the proofs. When she walked down the drive a little later, the sun was sinking on what had been a perfect spring day, and she was happy to be able to savour a little of it by walking home. Behind her, the long, low grey stone house took on a warmer look than usual in the oblique rays of the sun. Nearing the wide wrought-iron gates, she met Mrs. Midhurst, the housekeeper.

"Good-night," said Josephine with a smile.

"Good-night, Miss Riverton. If you should happen to see Barry on your way, would you tell him to come home at once? It's long past tea-time. I expect he's playing cricket on the green."

"It's still the football season, surely."

"As far as Barry's concerned, there is no game but cricket, whatever the time of the year. That's Bill Mendon's influence," she concluded severely.

"If I see him, I'll deliver the message," promised Josephine, thinking that it was no crime to interest a small boy in cricket, and that Bill Mendon, the gardener, was probably the only person at Valery Mount to take an interest in the housekeeper's son. Mrs. Midhurst kept Barry well out of Conrad's way, and doubtless ruled in her flat over the garage with the same severe efficiency with which she managed the household affairs of Valery Mount. Josephine had never come within miles of understanding what went on behind the cool reserve of the housekeeper. With a little more animation, more warmth, she would have been an attractive woman, with her fair hair framing an oval face with neat, regular features and large pale blue eyes. She was tall and slender, and Josephine guessed her to be in her late thirties. There was no doubting her competence, or her devotion to Conrad. Her devotion to her son was less evident. She nodded now and turned away up the drive with her brisk, straight-backed walk, and Josephine went on her way.

Five minutes walk down the lane brought her to Elmfield village green occupied by two boys and a dog. In front of two school satchels placed on top of a coat for a wicket, a thin dark-haired boy was batting. Bowling and fielding with more zeal than skill was a tubby little boy some years younger than the batsman. As Josephine approached them, the bowler was protesting.

"Let me have a bat now. You've been batting all the time."

"You should get me out, then," said the batsman with a wild swipe at the ball, which was a good yard off the

11

wicket, sending it skying towards the far boundary.

"You can get it. I'm tired," declared the fielder sulkily.

"Your ball. I don't care," said the batsman, resting on his bat.

As Josephine watched the protesting fielder amble after the ball with the peculiar rolling gait of a sailor, shoulders hunched, she reflected that Barry was a born loser. He would always be the toiler, the plums never for him. It took him so long to find the ball that the batsman decided not to wait. Picking up his satchel, he threw down the bat and walked off, a faintly derisive grin on his face as he waved to the distant figure scuffling round in the long grass by the fence. Josephine collected the remaining coat, satchel and bat and walked across the green. Barry, the ball found, ambled towards her, his plain freckled face despondent, his loose jersey and baggy shorts making him look even more podgy. His sandy coloured hair was so curly that it covered his head with what looked like tight brass springs, and was doubtless the subject of much teasing. Unprepossessing as his appearance and manner were, there was something about Barry Midhurst that went to Josephine's heart. Destined to be a butt, a protesting underdog, she felt the scales of life were unfairly weighted against him. His pugilistic attitude was, she was sure, the inevitable reaction of an eight year old child who was always at a disadvantage, and she had been rewarded once or twice by a piercingly sweet smile from the boy which suggested that inside that podgy figure lived a different person altogether. His expression now was far from sweet, however.

"I've been bowling and fielding all the time, and he never let me bat," he said.

"Too bad. You'd better hurry home now. Your mother

asked me to remind you that it's long past your tea-time."

She watched him for a minute, toiling back up the lane, his jacket trailing from one hand, swiping at the hedge with his bat as he went along, putting his plump legs down heavily at a tortoise-like pace.

The final stretch of Josephine's walk home consisted of an uphill climb along a footpath between high hedgerows, and she sat down to rest on a seat near the top which gave a view through a gap in the hedge across a sloping meadow and belt of woodland to a distant glimpse of the sea between a gap in the downs. The setting sun cast a mellow light over the scene, familiar to her for so many years, for she had climbed up and down this path to school and to the village, and knew it in all its seasons. Now the hazel trees were swinging their gold catkins once again, the hawthorn buds were just showing green, and lambs were bleating in the meadow below. And it was here on this seat that she had finally broken with Mike after a running battle that had started soon after she had begun working for Conrad Ravensburg and had stretched over several nerve-racking months to the final scene here on a June day nearly four years ago. And since then she had neither seen nor heard from him again. Mutual friends had avoided mentioning his name out of delicacy, she assumed. Then she had heard that he had left the district to join a firm of solicitors in London, a fact which had surprised her for he was Sussex born, as she was, and was a country-lover with no liking for city life. But perhaps he had felt the need for the wider experience of a London practice to further his career in the legal profession.

She had no regrets. At least, hardly any regrets, she thought, as she watched a lamb frisking round its imperturbable mother. She had been a child then. Much as she had enjoyed her girlhood friendship with Mike, sharing the countryside with him, accepting the way he had taken her over, there had come a time when she needed to assert her independence. His resentment of the claims Conrad made on her time had undermined their friendship from the start, but the past four years, when she had travelled widely, researching all sorts of projects, meeting a wide circle of interesting people, had proved infinitely rewarding and enriching, widening her horizons, bringing her a confidence she had never possessed before, until, looking back, it seemed that only in childhood had she known Mike Wexford, a childhood left far behind. She was happy in her work, and happy in her home, and loved the countryside she had been born in. Altogether, she thought, getting to her feet, she was a very lucky person, but a native caution within her wondered if she was tempting providence by admitting to such complacency.

She found her mother, as usual, in the garden, weeding among the wallflowers. She looked up, astonished as her daughter appeared.

"Good heavens! It can't be that late. Are you home early, darling?"

"Rather late, as a matter of fact."

"Well, it's a cold meal. Won't take me a minute to do a salad. I don't know where time goes to in the garden. Hasn't it been a lovely day? I'll just dead-head these daffodils. For once, they haven't been spoiled by rain, hail or gales. I remember one spring when they were buried up to their necks in snow."

"I'll do the salad," said Josephine as her mother stretched her back rather painfully. "Did you stop for tea?"

"Didn't realise the time."

Josephine shook her head.

"I shall come home one day and find you stretched out in the garden unconscious from exhaustion and lack of food."

"Dangerous to work on a full stomach, and I only need one meal a day at my age. By the way, dear, Sophie telephoned this morning just after you'd left. She and Guy are giving a little house-warming party next Saturday, and hope you'll be there. About six-thirty. Not to bother to let them know. Just turn up if you can."

"Oh good. I'm looking forward to seeing their new home. It's taken them long enough to find it. Sophie kept falling for picturesque ruins and Guy kept pointing out the snags. Guy is my favourite man and Sophie's a darling. Should be a jolly evening."

"You're looking very blooming this evening, dear. I like that grey and white outfit."

Josephine tucked her hand under her mother's arm as they walked indoors.

"I was seized by a rare feeling of euphoria as I walked home. Dangerously complacent. The effect of the first warm spring day, I guess."

"Ah, spring works wonders for the morale."

Afterwards, Josephine was to look back at that day as another turning point. The first had come four years earlier when she had broken with Mike, bringing to an end a happy companionship of many years, for she had known him when she was a schoolgirl and he, her senior by six years, the son of their doctor, who lived at the end of the lane. Perhaps that had been the trouble. He had taken her over, as it were, when the difference in their ages made that logical, and she had been content to follow his lead. At twenty, she had grown up and wanted to lead a life of her own. When she had joined Conrad Ravensburg, the pleasant meadows of the past years had become a battlefield culminating in a complete and final break with Mike. And that had marked the end of her girlhood. The years that followed had been interesting and rewarding and had brought her to that euphoric day of spring with no regrets for the past and a maturity and confidence which enabled her to look back at that shy, malleable teenager with faint wonder and amusement.

But on that evening in March, she had no premonition that the inevitable law of change was to make this another turning point in her life.

# 2
# *The Face of an Enemy*

Josephine arrived late at the party, for her car gave trouble again and it had taken a garage hand twenty minutes to find the fault and rectify it. As she had only the previous day collected the car and paid a handsome bill for its overhaul, her natural antipathy to machines was reinforced as she drove as fast as was safe along the narrow twisting lanes to the village of Deanswood and managed to find Cheriton Cottage just before dark. It looked old, with its lichen-bearing tiled roof and mellow bricks, latticed windows and deep eaves in the true Sussex tradition. She parked her car behind several tucked away down a side drive screened from the cottage by a high beech hedge, and walked round to the front gate and down the winding path to the oak-studded door over which a lamp shed its light, revealing the silver grey of the weathered wood. The air was full of the scent of wallflowers which bordered the path and filled the beds under the windows.

Sophie opened the door and welcomed Josephine with a delighted smile.

"Oh, you were able to make it, after all. I'm so glad, Jo. It was short notice, I know."

And then Guy was there, and she gave them the blue Venetian glass paper-weight which she had bought them, and Guy kissed her by way of thanks, saying,

"How very beguiling of you, Jo, to give us such a happy reminder of our honeymoon in Italy, where we first met you. Remember that shop just round the corner from the hotel where they had such beautiful glass? You haven't been saving it up ever since then, have you?"

"Hardly. I spotted this no further away than Fordingham."

"Well, bless you!"

With one arm round her and one round Sophie, Guy shepherded them into the noisy sitting-room. She knew most of the people there, and Sophie was introducing her to the few she did not know when she was brought up short by a dark-suited back and thick black hair. There was something familiar about those shoulders and the gesture of the hand as the man talked to his companion. He turned as Sophie touched his shoulder.

"Mike, can I introduce you to our friend, Josephine? Jo, this is Mike Wexford, who's just joined Guy in partnership."

And as Mike's dark blue eyes regarded her with interest, he said, with what seemed to her a faintly sardonic smile,

"Well, well. How are you, Josephine, after all this time?"

"You two know each other?"

"Yes," said Josephine, collecting herself. "Or we did, a long time ago, when we were very young."

"Well, I'll leave you to come up to date, then," said Sophie.

Josephine took a generous sip from her glass of sherry, needing time and a little stiffener in the face of this unexpected encounter from the past. His dark face was leaner, the rugged features more sharply defined, but the great difference was that this face, once so familiar to her, was now quite unreadable. In demeanour, he was a stranger. The volatile temperament, the fiery spirit, were now, it seemed, either quenched or under cast-iron control. The deep, attractive voice, once so charged with vitality, was now calm and measured as he said,

"Have you known Guy and Sophie long?"

"About eighteen months. I met them when they were having a belated honeymoon in Italy. I've never heard your name mentioned by them."

"Oh, mine's more of a business friendship with Guy. We met at a legal conference a year or so ago. I've only recently got to know Sophie."

"And you're joining Guy's practice?"

"Yes. As from last month."

"You were in the City, I believe."

"Yes."

Not exactly forthcoming, thought Josephine, trying again.

"I don't expect you were sorry to leave London. Where will you be living now?"

"I've bought Guy's flat in Fordingham. Overlooking the sea. But what of you, Josephine? Still working for the Great Man?"

"Yes."

"It appears to suit you," he said, his eyes going over her in a cool way that brought a flush to her cheeks.

"It does. I've found it a fascinating and rewarding job in every way."

"Congratulations," he said with a wry little smile as he turned away and moved across the room to join an elderly man sitting alone on a sofa in the corner.

Josephine, feeling as though she had just been on the receiving end of a bucket of cold water, joined some friends and was soon engaged in a friendly argument about contemporary music, for Guy and Sophie were both keen music-lovers and so were most of their friends. But underneath, she seethed at that cool brush-off from Mike, although why she should be annoyed at being treated with a modicum of politeness as though she was a stranger, she did not know, for they were strangers now. Too much water had flowed under the bridge during these past years for it to be otherwise. But need he have treated her as the sort of stranger encountered at a party from whom it was desirous to extricate oneself with as much speed as was consistent with politeness? Then her sense of humour reasserted itself. No reaction was quite so mortifying as complete indifference. Dislike, anger, even scorn, were more tolerable, signifying at least some sort of interest. But indifference was a chilling experience rare in her social life now, for if not for her own sake, her close connection with Conrad Ravensburg caused her to be sought out and flattered.

Adroitly, for the party was quite a small one, Mike managed to avoid any further conversation with her, but once or twice she caught him eyeing her with the brief, cool detachment of a man in a picture gallery facing a painting of no particular merit or appeal. He seemed to have made a great hit with Jean Brynton, the wife of Guy's closest friend, Darrel. She was a slender young woman with tawny hair and a warm personality, and as Josephine watched them laughing and talking across the room, she recognised in Mike the old vitality and charm that had been so hard to resist. Darrel and Sophie joined them and then, as though to clinch the argument they were all obviously enjoying, Jean held up her hand and began to sing a few bars. Mike put his arm round her shoulders and joined in. Above the conversation of the room it was impossible to recognise the music, but from Darrel's amusement, Sophie's helpless laughter and the histrionic gestures of Mike and Jean, she guessed that they were giving a parody of an operatic duet. Mike put the shutters up only for her, it seemed.

"Time we broke this up and adjourned for some food," said Guy's voice from behind her.

She gave him a warm smile.

"I love your cottage, Guy. It's welcoming and cosy. Low ceilings and latticed windows for me every time. They give a snug feeling of protection against all hostile elements, aided by Sophie's artistic eye for warm colours and flowers in odd corners. I wish it was light enough to see the garden. Is it a big one?"

"Just over an acre. Enough for Sophie to enjoy without flogging herself to death. She'll be the gardener here. I shall just do as I'm told, being sadly ignorant about things horticultural. Sophie tells me you know my new partner."

"Yes. We more or less grew up together. His father was our doctor. They lived just down the lane from us. We lost touch some years ago, though."

"An unusually good legal brain. I'm lucky to have persuaded him to join us. Heard him read a brilliant paper at a Law Society meeting last year. Now that Wadebridge is retiring, I'm very glad indeed to have gained such a capable partner. But I mustn't talk shop. Let's round this lot up and have some food."

The cold buffet supper which was laid in the dining-room and from which they all helped themselves was a joy to the eyes, thought Josephine, trying to choose between chicken, turkey, ham and a game pie. There were bowls of salad, dishes of hot baked potatoes in their jackets, crusty home-made bread, a variety of cheeses, bowls of fruit salad and two luscious-looking fruit flans.

"Looking at that, I feel decidedly hungry," said Darrel Brynton.

Guy poured wine or beer, according to taste, and it couldn't have been a happier party, thought Josephine, refusing to be affected by the skill with which Mike avoided all contact with her without appearing to do so. She might have been the invisible woman as far as he was concerned. Happily, a fair young giant called Derek Padstow attached himself to her and proved a pleasant companion, an enthusiasm for physical fitness and sporting activities of all kinds making conversation with him easy if not exciting. Over the cheese, however, he ceased talking about his enthusiasms and said,

"I say, is it true that you're Conrad Ravensburg's Girl Friday?"

"You could put it like that."

"What's it like, working for the famous?"

Josephine considered.

"Often arduous, always interesting, and demanding complete involvement. I enjoy it."

"He's an impressive chap. Not that I've read any of his books. Not a bookish person myself. But I've seen him on T.V. and he opened our new youth club last year. Went down very well. Decent of him, really, with so many calls on his time."

Josephine refrained from saying that Conrad considered all such functions good publicity, and sipped her coffee while this ingenuous and keen young man went on from admiring Conrad, who had evidently made a great impression on him, to telling her about his job as a physical education teacher at a training college near Fordingham.

22

He stayed close to her for most of the remainder of the evening, having it seemed few interests in common with the rest of the party, and although it was impossible to dislike such a good-natured young man, it was with some relief that she welcomed Darrel Brynton's intervention later on.

"Come upstairs, Josephine, and see some of the botanical drawings Sophie has done for our journal. Guy thinks you'd be interested."

As she followed him upstairs to the room which Sophie used as a studio, he said,

"Guy's idea. He thought you were a bit bogged down with Derek and could do with a change."

"I'd love to see the drawings," she said happily.

She liked the tall dark Dr. Darrel Brynton, who was the head of a Horticultural Station, and although her knowledge of things horticultural, like Guy's, was limited, she had imbibed a little from her mother's enthusiasm, and studied the fine line drawings of alpine plants with interest and admiration.

"They're beautifully drawn. Sophie really is gifted, isn't she?"

"Yes. Her father was a great botanist, and Sophie inherited his love of plants."

"This really does feel a happy home," said Josephine, putting down the last of the drawings. "As though Guy and Sophie have lived here, happy and busy, for years. It fits them so well."

"Yes. A good match in every way. Sophie was overdue for some happiness. She went through a very bad time before Guy rescued her. Now, I wonder whether your watchdog has turned his attention elsewhere. A good chap, but a little heavy-handed."

"Doesn't seem quite to fit in with Guy and Sophie," she said as they walked downstairs to join the others.

"They have an indulgent affection for him. I've never understood quite why, but then Sophie has a tender heart, and she's had a remarkably softening effect on Guy, who used to share my sin of not suffering fools gladly, and is now more tolerant than I could ever be."

And Darrel, determined to save her from being engulfed by Derek again, pushed her straight into the arms of Mike, standing alone by the bookcase, studying the contents. Derek was sitting with Mr. Wadebridge, glass in hand, listening to his companion with a bored expression, his eyes roving round the room. The others were gathered round the record player where Guy was demonstrating the skill of a virtuoso horn player to prove some point, and called upon Darrel to give his opinion.

"Mike, look after Jo, will you? She's in need of care and protection from Derek's obsession with physical education. At any moment, he's going to have her doing press-ups or running round the garden ten times," said Darrel, leaving them.

Out of the frying pan into the fire, thought Josephine, her mouth beginning to go out of control and her eyes laughing as her sense of the absurd got the better of her.

"It doesn't occur to Darrel that you might prefer the press-ups," said Mike.

"Or that you might prefer the books."

"The choice to the lady. Or is that an anachronism in this day of women's lib?"

"But you never subscribed to that, did you?"

"In principle, yes."

"It never showed," she said demurely.

"You weren't looking in the right direction, perhaps.

24

None of the Great Man's books here. But then he's not written many books, considering the size of his reputation."

"It's quality not quantity that counts."

"And a good publicity manager."

"You still resent him?" she said, trying to hide her anger.

"Not in the least. It's all academic now. In fact, I must congratulate you on your transformation into a most attractive and polished young woman. A credit to Ravensburg's training, if I may say so."

"Transformation. I don't think I much care for that word. Transformation from what, may I ask?"

"Why, from an unsophisticated, gauche young girl. What else?"

His eyes mocked her.

"You're too kind," she said sweetly. "An ignorant child would be more accurate, perhaps."

"I can't accept that. But I'm sure you'll understand why I've no wish to be reminded of the past. Time brings changes. Let me say, quite objectively, that I appreciate the present gloss. Some of Ravensburg's reflected glory surrounds you now, and is very agreeable, I'm sure."

"Yes, time does bring changes. Not for the better in your case, it seems. You always had a fiery temper but malicious sarcasm was never one of your weapons."

And she was amazed and startled at the anger that burned in his eyes at her words. He kept his voice low but it was charged with contempt as he said,

"You've a nerve, charging *me* with malice." Then he masked his anger with an icy formality. "I'm sorry our paths have crossed again. If I'd known you were to be here, I'd have made an excuse not to come. I'll leave you to find a more appreciative companion."

She watched him join a dark, slender woman on the far side of the room, whom Josephine had not known before that evening. She was a writer of detective stories named Hester Northbridge and she welcomed Mike with a smile and a quick babble of speech as though they knew each other well. Josephine's eyes dwelt on Mike's back with a feeling of stunned disbelief. He hated her. He really hated her. Thinking back over all those years of their youthful friendship, she could not believe it.

For the remainder of the evening, she pushed her shock and distress into the background, and not until she was driving home did she allow her mind to dwell on it. Too restless to go to bed when she arrived home, she put the car away and walked down the garden. The moon was full, the sky cloudless, and the night was still. She sat on the seat by the pool and stared at the fronds of the willow tree just putting forth their trailing leaves, and saw nothing but the hatred burning in those dark blue eyes. It was not possible. Reproach, coolness, perhaps. But hatred?

Malice, he had said. But there had never been malice between them. Arguments, quarrels during the last six months of their engagement, but never malice. And was it such a crime to break an engagement? She thought back over that last six months. It was true that her new job had demanded much of her leisure time as well as her working hours. There had been a lot of socialising. Cocktail parties, luncheons in town, to which Conrad had taken her, insisting that she got to know his large circle of friends and acquaintances, all part of her job, he had said. And then, when she and Mike had planned a holiday in

Wales, Conrad had whisked her away to Greece, where he wanted her assistance in doing some research there for the background of a book. And after that, the last straw for Mike, had come the six months' trip to Switzerland, where Conrad had stayed with friends in their lakeside chalet and she had stayed at a small hotel nearby while they worked on the book with the Greek setting. He always worked well in Switzerland, he maintained. The air suited him. And Greek food did not. It had all been arranged in something of a rush, and a few days after that row with Mike when she had told him that her job came first, she had been on the plane to Zurich, so that there had been little time for second thoughts.

It had been a strange interlude, that visit to Switzerland. She had never travelled at all before joining Conrad, and her delight and excitement at the magnificent scenery and different way of life in Switzerland had been shot through with dismay and regrets about her break with Mike, so that it was something of a mixed tapestry of experience. In her heart, she had hoped that they might mend matters on her return, perhaps establish the old easy friendship without Mike making so many demands of her. In fact, she thought now as she watched the reflection of the moon in the water, she had wanted the best of both worlds. Her relationship with Mike was so old-established, she had never really envisaged an absolute break.

But when they arrived back, she found that Mike had moved to London, that his father had retired and moved to Cornwall, the county of his birth, and their new addresses were unknown. And with the scope of her work for Conrad increasing and her interest and enthusiasm for her job not flagging, she had put Mike out of mind

27

most of the time, only feeling a little ache occasionally. So why should she now be so distressed at the unexpected encounter that evening? If she felt shocked at the violent change in his feelings towards her, then she should congratulate herself on escaping from the arms of a man whose nature had unpleasant aspects which she had never known. But it was not like Mike, she thought. Not venom and malice. He was not small-minded. Volatile, yes. But fair-minded. Hurt pride? Vanity? Could they be behind his vehement rejection of even a civil manner towards her?

Round and round went her thoughts, until, tired and cold, she told herself angrily that she was well rid of such a man, and that it was foolish to bemoan an old friendship spoiled. It belonged to a shadowy past, when she was a child. It had no reality now. She would forget it.

Creeping quietly upstairs, she saw the light under her mother's bedroom door, and looked in. Her mother had been reading, and she looked over her glasses at her daughter.

"Hullo, darling. Had a good evening?"

"Lovely. Tell you about it in the morning."

"I heard the car. You've been a long time."

"M'm. A lovely night. I lingered in the garden. Guy and Sophie have a dream of a cottage. By the way, guess who was there?" she added, knowing she would have to reveal it sooner or later but feeling reluctant even to mention his name. "Mike. Michael Wexford."

"That was a surprise."

"You're telling me. He's just joined Guy as a partner. He's living in Fordingham now. Bought Guy's flat."

"Oh," said her mother, looking thoughtful. "Any tremors?"

"I hardly recognised him," said Josephine lightly.

"The door's quite locked on the past. Odd, though, wasn't it? Coming across him again like that. What have you been reading?"

She picked up the book. A collection of Thomas Hardy's poems. Her eyes were caught by the title of a poem on the open page. 'Paths of Former Time'. It was quite short, and her eyes scanned it quickly. She went back and read out the last two verses.

> Had you been
> Sharer of that scene
> You would not ask while it bites in keen
>
> Why it is so
> We can no more go
> By the summer paths we used to know!

"M'm. Nice," she said. "Nice, but sad. You know, you shouldn't stay awake for me whenever I'm out in the car. I'm the world's most careful driver."

"I know, dear. I can't help it. And, anyway, I'm glad of the opportunity for a quiet read. Never seem to get much time during the day."

Josephine smiled and kissed her good-night. The photograph of her father on the bedside table was a constant reminder to her mother of the hazards of the road, for he had died after a long struggle to survive a car accident. Six years ago, she thought, when the paths of summer had come to an end for her mother.

In her room, she stared at herself in the mirror. Glossy? She looked at her reflection as though at a stranger to see if it appeared to warrant the term he had used, and saw a slender figure in a jade green dress, the only ornament a

29

silver chain. An oval face, dark brown hair, straight and thick, curved smoothly round the face to swing bell-like just clear of the shoulders, dark brown eyes, straight nose, wide mouth drooping a little with tiredness, rather pale. Glossy? She thought not. But, once she had known Mike was present, she had put on an extra bright front instinctively, by way of defence. What Conrad called her 'Into Battle' charm, guaranteed to disarm and conquer the most suspicious V.A.T. inspector or complaining agent. She turned away impatiently. It had been a thoroughly disturbing evening, and she was angry that Mike had effectively spoilt for her what should have been a very happy occasion. She would give him no further thought.

But in bed, sleep eluded her, and he would not be dismissed. The paths of summer. She kept remembering the old days with him. The walks on the downs, the trips to the coast for a swim when it was hot, the excitement over Mike's first old banger of a car. Picnics, bird-watching, the occasional celebration with a dinner and dance in one of the Fordingham hotels. But it was mostly in the countryside where their happiest hours had been spent. Somehow, life had seemed so simple then. Their companionship easy and natural. Until their engagement. They should never have taken that step, she thought. She was too young, Mike became too possessive. The gap of six years between them at that stage became more marked The paths of summer. The phrase haunted her. Those particular paths, she thought, were closed to her for ever. Mike had made that abundantly clear. And she couldn't have found her way back, anyway. She had moved on. And so had he. Strangers now. As far as Mike was concerned, enemies. The shock of that was still with her as she drifted uneasily into sleep.

# 3
# *Brief Encounters*

The fair days of March were succeeded by spiteful days of April, with cold winds and frequent showers, and Josephine welcomed a particularly busy period of work to help keep thoughts of Mike at bay and make the disappointing weather less relevant to her life since she would have had little time to enjoy the spring out of doors even had it been the kind of April Robert Browning dreamed of. For Conrad was writing a play. Only the second he had attempted. The first had been a failure, long since forgotten. This was a historical play, involving much research on Josephine's part, hours of discussion with the likely producer, and anguish on the part of Conrad's agent which spilled over Josephine's head, for Conrad had a masterly way of being elusive when Brian Renfrow came on the scene.

"Terribly sorry, my dear chap. Have to rush up to London. Can only spare a few minutes. Josephine will put you in the picture and relay any points you want to make. Seeing this producer for a natter about casting."

This was the latest excuse when Renfrow arrived one morning, having made what he thought was a definite appointment with Conrad. Renfrow was not amused.

"If you were going up to London, why the heck didn't you phone me and we could have met in my office afterwards? Why drag me down here because you didn't want to interrupt your work, and then go to London after all?"

"It *is* my work, Brian, and it wasn't fixed until this morning, too late to let you know. So sorry, my dear chap, but Josephine knows all about everything and can stand in for me. You know she's my *alter ego*. Help yourself to a drink."

And Brian Renfrow heaved a sigh of resignation as he poured himself a whisky and watched Conrad's departure from the window.

"God give me patience," he said. "Why on earth is he going in for this sort of caper, Josephine? It's not his line. His publisher's pressing for his next book, and where is it?"

"Languishing, with only two chapters completed and no clear idea of what's to follow."

He sat down in an armchair, and nursed his glass in silence for a few moments, frowning. Josephine had always got on well with this thin, balding man with the lugubrious expression and shrewd eyes. He had been Conrad's agent from the beginning, and a seesaw relationship existed between them, Conrad all charm and appreciation as far as words went, and going his own way without paying any heed to his agent as far as action went. But Renfrow was unsparing in protecting and promoting Conrad's interests and his judgment in literary matters was widely respected.

"Do you think he's played out?" he asked bluntly.

"No. Certainly not. After all, he's not that old, and his talent with words is as good as ever, I'm sure."

"Sixty-eight. Doesn't look it, of course. Health's marvellous. But he seems to me to be writing ever more beautifully about less and less. Words for the sake of words. And now messing about with drama, not his line at all. He needs space for his writing. Hasn't created a dramatic character in his life. All subtlety and sensibility. He's wasting his time."

"I think he felt he needed a change."

"Restless. Application seems lacking these days. And writing's largely a matter of application, you know. He's passing more and more of the donkey work on to you. Was a time when he wouldn't have trusted anybody within a mile of his work. Secretaries, of course. But just for the typing. Doesn't seem to me to be so involved, and it shows. Without you, now, I guess he'd be sunk."

"No, Mr. Renfrow. You exaggerate."

He shook his head.

"Well, we all have to get old, I suppose. Don't let him eat up your life to prolong his own career, my dear."

"His name is made. He could rest on his laurels now if he wished. A great writer."

Renfrow considered this for a few moments.

"A good writer. Not great. A real talent for words. And a marvellous self-promoter. He's created his own image and put it over with consummate skill, aided by my son, who knows all about the value of publicity."

Renfrow's voice was dry and he regarded his whisky morosely.

"I'm sorry Conrad's wasted your time this morning. Can I get any message through for you?" asked Josephine.

"I doubt it. Try to get him to think about the new novel if you can, but once he starts chasing hares, no advice of mine will deflect him."

"I don't think you're enjoying that drink. Shall I make some coffee? I could do with a cup."

"Thanks, my dear. Too early in the day for whisky. Don't know why I took it. Why does one always fall in with Conrad's suggestions?"

"One is swept away by the charm."

"Not I. Not after all these years. But, confound it, perhaps I am in rare moments of weakness. I think it's time I retired and left the business to John. He understands this modern world. I don't. I used to think it was the merit of literary work itself that counted, but it seems that publicity, building the image, getting in with the right trendy fashion, are what count. Time I got out and turned to gardening or keeping bees."

"This weather's enough to depress anybody. I'll get some coffee. I keep all the equipment at hand without troubling Mrs. Midhurst, since Conrad needs copious supplies to keep him going."

Over coffee, Renfrow gave her details of an offer for subsidiary rights for Conrad's consideration.

"If he can bring his mind to bear on it, perhaps he'll give me a ring tomorrow," he said as he closed his brief-case. "There were one or two matters I wanted to discuss about his next contract, but they can wait. You're looking tired, my dear. Don't let him wear you out. The old monster uses people, you know."

"I've no complaints. I've enjoyed these past years, and he's been very good to me."

"You're invaluable to him. You've got talent yourself."

"I've learned a lot from Conrad."

He nodded, and as she saw him off, he patted her shoulder and said,

"In a way, I suppose we're both in the same boat. Take care of yourself."

Surprised and a little touched by this show of affection from a man as dry and undemonstrative as Brian Renfrow, she watched him walk to his car, and waved him off. He looked tired, she thought. And that made two of them.

But it was less the busy spell of work than the gnawing knowledge of Mike's hostility that was wearing, for her scant leisure was haunted by him.

Her next encounters with him did nothing to reassure her. The first was in Dilford, the town some ten miles from Elmfield, where she had sought out the public library one Saturday morning to check some references. It was a thriving little town, and she was reminded of Mike again when she passed the offices of the solicitors where he had worked as an articled clerk and then assistant before he had left for London. She had met him there once or twice when they were going to a concert, for Dilford held a music festival each year. It was with difficulty that she dismissed him from her mind and concentrated on her researches. Then, coming out of the library about an hour later, she saw him on the other side of the road, a parcel under his arm. He was right opposite her, waiting to cross. Dodging a bus, watching the traffic, he arrived within a couple of yards of her before he recognised her.

"Hullo, Mike," she said.

And he walked past her as though she was invisible. It was the first time anybody had cut her, and her cheeks flushed as she turned away and walked in the opposite direction, scarcely conscious of where she was going until she realised that it was away from the car park where she had left her car.

At the second encounter, he was unable to cut her. She had driven into Fordingham one sunny day in May to stock up with some office equipment, and, having dumped her parcels in the car, she made for a little restaurant not far from the sea front. It was full, but as she looked round the crowded room, a voice hailed her and she turned to see the dark, quirky face of Hester Northbridge. She had to think a moment, and then remembered. The writer of detective stories she had met at Guy's house-warming. Sitting opposite her was Mike.

"No room at the inn, unless you share our table. You're welcome," she said, with a smile.

It was impossible to decline without seeming unfriendly, however stony the expression on Mike's face as he rose while Josephine seated herself next to Hester. They were well on with their meal, she noticed.

"I need another female to help me cope with this male chauvinist," said Hester cheerfully. "He's the worst cynic I know where women are concerned."

"You, my dear Hester, are the exception to all strictures," said Mike with an urbanity he never used to have at his disposal.

"Because I'm plain, shall never see my thirties again, and prefer writing to matrimony, so pose no threat."

"Ah, but you have a keen intelligence, and that's a strong weapon. Looks are irrelevant, but I rather take to yours. A lively challenge there."

"I need all the resources of my intelligence to keep you in order. The worst of a lawyer is that argument is meat and drink to him. By the way, I wouldn't recommend the omelettes. Like old flannel," Hester observed as Josephine scanned the menu.

She ordered a cheese salad and asked Mike politely whether he was comfortable in Guy's old flat. He answered equally politely that he was.

"He's nice and quiet down there," said Hester, who occupied the flat above. "Guy used to be addicted to playing his records of Wagner's *Ring* or Verdi's *Otello* at full blast. Eventually, we came to an amicable arrangement about our respective noise-making activities, because my typewriter reverberates somewhat."

"These modern blocks need better sound-proofing, but they make for comfortable living," observed Mike. "Now, if you'll excuse me, I'll skip coffee. I'm in court this afternoon and need to look over some papers first."

Neatly done, thought Josephine, as he nodded and left them.

Hester asked her about Conrad and her work, and Josephine learned something of Hester's career as they chatted on, Josephine at ease now that Mike had gone. Over coffee, however, Hester brought up that thorny subject.

"Mike Wexford's an interesting character. Not that I've been able to extract a great deal, but I like him although he keeps his feelings on ice. But my word, he's been badly burned by some female in the past. Bitter as gall. You knew him when you were kids, didn't Sophie say?"

"Yes. His father knew mine."

"Know what gave him frost-bite?"

"It was burns just now."

Hester grinned.

"I exercise more care about mixing my metaphors when I'm writing. I'll stick to frosted. Any clues?"

"I lost touch some years ago," said Josephine, wishing that Hester would remove her enquiring mind from Mike.

"And probably think it's none of my business, anyway. It's an occupational disease, you know. Curiosity about what makes people tick. Most writers suffer from it, I guess."

"And the fruits go into your books and make them so convincing. I've just read your last. Characters that really come alive."

And that kept the conversation in safe channels until they parted outside the restaurant.

"Come along one evening soon and we can have a long natter about books and writers. You must have come across a lot in that august literary sphere your employer adorns."

"Thanks. I'll do that," said Josephine, warming to the lively personality of Hester Northbridge.

But as she walked back to her car, the chilling fact that Mike had locked and barred the door against her was inescapable, and her anger at his treatment was laced with a feeling that somehow, somewhere, she had gone wrong.

Helping her mother with some weeding in the garden that evening, she said suddenly,

"Mother, did you ever talk to Dr. Wexford about Mike and me after our engagement was broken off? While I was in Switzerland."

Her mother looked up, a length of bindweed trailing from her hand.

"No, dear. There was no opportunity. I had a feeling he was avoiding me. Felt a little embarrassed by it, perhaps, although I would never have thought him a man easily embarrassed, and we'd known him for years. Perhaps I was mistaken, though. On the one or two occasions when I saw him, he was probably in a hurry to get to a patient. Then I heard that he'd retired and gone to live in Cornwall."

"A bit sudden, wasn't it? The village must have known beforehand. Didn't you hear anything?"

"Well, you know I'm a bit of a recluse. I don't go to the village often and I've never been a mixer in local activities, so I don't really know much of what goes on."

Josephine nodded and started to tug at a dandelion. It

was true that her mother's heart and mind had been given entirely to her home and family, her garden and the countryside, and she had become even more anti-social since she had been widowed, as though shrinking from the well-meant sympathy of acquaintances.

"All the same," said Josephine, "I'd have thought he'd have come to tell you and say goodbye. After all, he was an old friend of Dad's, and of all of us. My action in breaking off the engagement wasn't criminal."

"I confess I was a little surprised. Why do you ask, Jo? It's all ancient history now."

"M'm. So it is."

"What's bothering you?"

Josephine hesitated, then said slowly,

"Mike's attitude to me on the few occasions we've met lately has been so bitter, so hostile."

"Well, I suppose rejection is hard to accept gracefully. He was very fond of you, Jo."

"I know. So was I of him. Marriage means a bit more than that, though. I had the right to choose. And the way Mike behaved those last few months, it seemed the right decision for him, too."

"You're surely not in any doubt about it now, are you?"

"No. No doubt at all."

"Then why worry about it?"

"It's not quite as simple as that. Mike joining Guy as a partner has resulted in our having mutual friends and acquaintances and we're bound to run across each other occasionally. I don't see why we can't meet in a civilised, friendly manner. But Mike treats me like an enemy, someone who has injured him maliciously. It's not like him. He was never a petty person. There's something. . ."

She sought in vain to pin it down in words. "Something

39

wrong somewhere. I feel it. Something I don't understand. Or perhaps I'm imagining things. Perhaps Mike wasn't the fair-minded person I thought he was. He certainly didn't behave like one latterly. Perhaps he was always arrogant, and furious when thwarted. I wouldn't know. I never went against him until I joined Conrad and he resented the claims of my job."

She had been twisting the offending dandelion in her hands until it was crushed and limp.

"I wouldn't start analysing the past now," said her mother briskly. "You can never go back. And I really can't see the point of your working up a feeling of guilt just because Mike has appeared on the scene again with a less agreeable face. Ignore it. You're only likely to meet him in company with others. That shouldn't present any difficulty. You can smooth over any awkwardness, I'm sure. You're so well equipped socially now."

"Glossy, would you say?"

"Not glossy, dear," said her mother, surprised at the unusual edge to her daughter's voice. "Only a charming assurance which I have never possessed and which I envy. At least, I don't envy it now. But when I was young, social occasions were agony to me. Gauche, awkward, quite hopeless. Some of your poise would have been a godsend."

"But think what you've been spared by eschewing social occasions. You know that even if you'd possessed the knack, you'd have been bored stiff. And Dad would never have fallen in love with you, because he hated social occasions even more than you. A real pair of shirkers, you two."

"Yes, we lived in a private world of our own. But a very happy one. So we didn't need to seek pleasure or distraction outside. What a burgeoning of growth there is in May! It's beautiful and heart-warming, but difficult to contain. I'll remove this lot to the compost heap."

Josephine watched her mother bear the trug full of weeds to the compost heap at the end of the garden. Even now, she could not bear to talk of her husband for long. Theirs had been a rare marriage of true minds, and Josephine, brought up in its warmth, had only fully appreciated it when she saw what bereavement did to her mother. Even now, after six years, sadness often looked out of her eyes, although she maintained a cheerful, practical front for her daughter's sake. She had refused to leave this house and the garden which she and David Riverton had made together, their first and only home, but Josephine sometimes wondered whether a change of scene would not have helped her mother. This garden was a kind of living memorial to her father, but her mother was still too young at fifty-eight to give her life over to a memorial of past happiness. Thinking of the terrible stunned grief of those first months of her mother's widowhood, Josephine remembered how kind Dr. Wexford had been all through her father's fight to live, and afterwards, and that brought her mind back to Mike. Bother the man, she thought. He wasn't worth her worrying. A man with the pride of Lucifer, unable to forget his resentment at being turned down. She was well rid of him. And she wouldn't allow him to drive her away from her friends for fear of meeting him, nor allow his hostility to spoil her enjoyment on those occasions when he was unfortunately present.

When Joyce Riverton returned to the scene of action, she found her daughter tugging angrily at a stubborn thistle as though she hated it.

# 4
# *Cricket Match*

Walking down the drive of Valery Mount one warm evening at the end of May, Josephine stopped to watch a large bumble bee force his way into the bell-shaped flower of a pink foxglove. Above the buzzing, she heard a snuffling noise coming from behind a clump of rhododendrons, and walking round to investigate, she found Barry half hidden among the bushes, prone on the ground, crying.

"Hullo there. What's wrong?"

He lifted a tear-stained, grubby face, and sniffed before turning aside, muttering "Nothing."

Josephine held out her hand.

"Come on. Get up and tell me."

"Mr. Mendon was going to take me to Fordingham tomorrow to see the county cricket team. But he's fallen off a ladder and his ankle's broke, and we can't go."

"His ankle's broken," corrected Josephine. "Poor Mr. Mendon."

"Mum won't let me go on my own," said Barry, with scant sympathy for Bill Mendon.

"Well, it's quite a long way to go. You'll be able to see them play some other time."

He glared at her, as though affronted by her stupidity.

"It's the only time they'll be playing at the Fordingham ground this season."

"Well, there's bound to be a village match on tomorrow. You'll probably enjoy that as much."

This was going from bad to worse. She was evidently sinking to awful depths in Barry's estimation. He spoke slowly, with scorn, in a voice made adenoidal by his recent tears.

"That's not first class cricket."

"I'm sorry, Barry. It's hard luck."

He sniffed, hunched his shoulders and walked off, brassy curls gleaming in the evening sunlight, too fat, wearing shorts several sizes too big, his grey shirt stained with grass and dirt, the picture of dejection. He'd be in trouble with his mother over the state of his shirt, and why on earth Mrs. Midhurst dressed him in such long baggy shorts she did not know. All very well to allow for growing, but not to look ahead for five or six years and make the child appear ludicrous.

"Barry," she called, and beckoned him as he turned. He came back slowly, still tearful. "I'll take you tomorrow, if your mother has no objection. Let's go and ask her."

His face was transformed in an instant, then he said, as though scarcely believing it,

"Would you? Would you really?"

"I've said so."

It was obvious that Barry Midhurst had no expectation that anyone would ever put themselves out for him except Bill Mendon, and Josephine rubbed his curls and said cheerfully,

"Clean up your face and hands, and brush yourself down. And look cleaner than that when you come with me tomorrow. I'm fussy about the passengers in my car."

And she was rewarded by that piercingly sweet smile that always caught her by surprise.

Mrs. Midhurst raised no objection.

"It's very good of you, Miss Riverton, I'm sure. I hope

you know what you're letting yourself in for."

"I'll survive. What time does play start, Barry?"

"Eleven o'clock."

"I'll be outside here at ten. Mind you're ready."

"He'll be ready. Late for everything else, but when it's cricket or Bill Mendon, it's another story. And just look at that shirt, my boy."

Josephine said goodbye and left them. She was doubtless in for a very boring day, for she knew little about cricket and had never felt drawn to learning more, but Barry Midhurst deserved a break sometimes. And if she wasn't to earn his scorn, she would have to dredge up some of her scanty knowledge of cricket lore to get her by. Her sole experience as a spectator was limited to two summers when Mike had played for the village team. She had been a schoolgirl of fourteen that first summer, and Mike a lordly twenty, treating her then with the teasing friendliness of an adult towards the kid down the lane who happened to be the daughter of his father's friend. It was not until two years later that the friendliness had taken on a warmer tone, and then studying for exams combined with an interest in Josephine Riverton had left him no time for cricket, and that had been the end of his cricketing career. All she could recall of those early cricketing days was seeing him hit a six over the pavilion to loud cheers, and joining in the search for the ball which had landed in a thicket of gorse and blackberries, and the game had been held up for some time before scratched hands and arms found it. It was not what Barry termed first class cricket. It would be just Barry's luck, she thought, if it poured with rain all day tomorrow.

But the next day dawned with a cloudless blue sky, and Barry was sitting on the gate of Valery Mount when she drew up. He looked as though he had been there for hours, for he climbed down very stiffly, picked up his cricket bat and tennis ball, and presented himself with a well scrubbed face, clean shirt and blazer over the same baggy shorts.

"You're not going to offer to play for them, are you?" asked Josephine as he settled himself beside her.

"In the intervals, we can play. All the boys play in the intervals. And I want to get the captain to autograph my bat."

"Well, it's going to be a very jolly day, I can see," said Josephine as she drove down the lane and headed for Fordingham.

The ground was at the back of the town, and bunting over the gates proclaimed that it was Fordingham Cricket Week. It took her some time to find a space to park her car, several minutes walk from the ground, but inside the ground they found two deckchairs in front of the refreshment pavilion which gave them an excellent side-on view. Barry insisted on having a score card, drew out his ball point pen, and hunched forward in his chair as his heroes came out. The home county was batting and Josephine leaned back and prepared to relax while Barry, aided by a friendly old gentleman on his left, proceeded to record every single thing that took place. She couldn't quite see the necessity for this, since the score board on the opposite side of the field clearly gave all the salient facts, but then the finer points of cricket lore were a mystery to her and she cloaked her ignorance by passing very few comments, merely smiling her thanks to the old gentleman who was evidently one of the initiated and whose experience went back into the distant past, although not as far back as W.G. Grace, as he made clear

45

when Barry asked him if he had ever seen that famous man bat. It was soon borne in on Josephine that a considerable amount of Bill Mendon's time in the garden had been given over to the education of Barry in cricketing history.

The sun was warm, the crowd cheerful, the home team batted well, their opponents from Leicester were an excellent fielding side, the ground was pleasing with its fringe of old trees and the church spire visible beyond them, and altogether it was a happy English summer scene, thought Josephine, half closing her eyes and missing the fall of a wicket.

They queued up for sandwiches and lemonade and coffee during the luncheon interval, followed by an ice cream for Barry, after which he ambled off to the area of grass behind the stand where some boys were playing their own brand of cricket. Josephine stood by the entrance to the pavilion, sipping her coffee, and watched him hover by the boys, bat and tennis ball in hand. After a few minutes, he said something to the boy nearest him, who looked at him and laughed and said something that sent Barry away. He walked slowly across the grass with his sailor's roll to two younger boys who were playing on their own. But his overtures were rejected there, too, with a rather less light-hearted response. As Barry retreated again, she heard one of the boys shout after him,

"Buzz off, Curly, and tie your trousers up."

How cruel boys were, she thought angrily, and prepared to sacrifice the rest of her coffee and go and bowl to Barry when a tall, broad-shouldered man caught the boy's arm and drew him off to an empty space beyond the other would-be cricketers. There, he proceeded to bowl gentle over-arm balls to Barry, who wielded his bat with more enthusiasm than skill, and obligingly fielded himself when he missed, as he frequently did. Then Mike was instructing him in the art of batting, changing his grip, putting him sideways on, demonstrating with Barry's junior-sized bat. She shifted back further into the shade of the refreshment pavilion, half screened by a wooden pillar, and watched them, oddly moved at the sight of the man she had been trying to dismiss as harsh and arrogant showing his old generosity of spirit when he saw a small, unprepossessing boy being ostracised. He kept up the instruction until the bell rang warning the public to clear the playing area, when he gave Barry a pat on the shoulder and left him, making for the stand behind the wicket. She walked behind him, shielded by the crowd, to join Barry already back at their chairs, but Mike had met someone he knew and stood chatting for a little time only a few yards in front of their seats.

"That man," said Barry excitedly as she slid into her chair, "he bowled to me. Showed me how to drive and cut. He knows ever such a lot about cricket."

"That was kind of him. I hope you thanked him."

"Yes. Yes, I think I did," he added doubtfully, as though in the excitement of having had someone to bowl for him, he could not be sure what he had said. "Perhaps I'd better go and do it again," he added as Mike and his friend parted, and he ran after him and she heard him say, "Thank you, sir. Thank you very much."

Mike looked amused and said, "That's all right, son. Mind you practise keeping a straight bat." Then he looked up and saw her, and the smile was wiped from his face on the instant. He made no gesture of recognition beyond a tightening of the lips and a brief nod. Then he strode off.

No generosity for her, she thought, and felt some of the sunshine of that day depart.

The afternoon session she found decidedly dull, for the home side, after losing two quick wickets, played with caution, and she was unable to keep her thoughts from straying to Mike, deeply troubled by his attitude to her. Undistracted by her companion, for Barry and the old gentleman were absorbed in the game, static or not, and Barry was concentrating on filling in his score card with a care he never gave to his lessons at school, Josephine worried at the problem like a dog trying to find meat on a bone, but with little satisfaction. Why so implacably hostile? Why did the fire of his resentment burn so fiercely after four years?

At the tea interval, Barry even sacrificed his tea to hang about the pavilion in the hope of getting his hero's autograph on his bat.

"Bill Mendon said that he usually comes out in the tea interval to sign autographs," he said, and forthwith planted himself at the foot of the steps leading to the players' pavilion. Josephine went off to the refreshment pavilion for a cup of much needed tea, and watched from a distance the tall fair county captain emerge from the players' pavilion. On the instant, it seemed, a queue of boys had formed up the steps, Barry, as usual, nearly last. The tea interval was over by the time he had reached the top of the queue, but he got his autograph and returned beaming to his chair, where Josephine had assembled some sandwiches, a cake and some lemonade for him.

"Look," he said proudly, and she duly admired the signature scrawled across the top end of the face of the bat. His cup of joy was full, and brushed by his happiness,

Josephine put the thorny subject of Mike behind her and prepared to enjoy the last session.

Driving home, though, it was that hard closed expression on Mike's face that stayed with her. A locked door. She would only bruise her hands if she tried to open it. Barry, tired out by the excitement, was dozing beside her, his bat clasped across his lap, the score card saved for Bill Mendon sticking out of his blazer pocket. It had not been a wasted day, she thought, as she drew up outside Valery Mount. Barry tumbled out and gave her his rare sweet smile as he thanked her, then he noticed Conrad walking down the drive, the smile vanished, and he ran off through the shrubbery towards the garage flat.

Conrad, letter in hand, leaned in at the open window of the car.

"Hullo, my dear. I hear from Mrs. Midhurst that you've been playing the good Samaritan to that child. I hope it wasn't too much of an ordeal."

"Not at all. I quite enjoyed the day."

He raised his eyebrows.

"Flannelled fools or muddied oafs. Never have decided which bore me most. Perhaps the flannelled fools are preferable since they are cleaner and less frenetic. Hardly to your taste either, I'm sure, so it was more than kind of you to give up your free time. I trust the boy behaved himself. Mrs. Midhurst does her best, but the material is pretty poor, I fear."

For once, she found Conrad's urbane detachment irritating.

"I enjoyed it because Barry enjoyed it so much. He behaved very well."

"That does great credit to your kind nature, my dear. I've a few friends looking in for drinks about eight this evening. Why not join us and finish the day in a civilised manner? All people you know. One of your most fervent admirers is coming, too. Young Cary Pearston. Remember? He rang me up this morning. He's on a touring holiday here. I invited him to stay over until tomorrow. He'll be delighted to renew your acquaintance. Asked after you."

She had to think a moment.

"The young American. Yes, I remember. A very keen young man."

"They all are. A nice lad. So do come, Josephine."

"I'm sorry, Conrad, but I really do feel tired," she said, hesitating.

"Nothing that a bath and change won't put right, I'm sure. It's short notice, but I only organised it this morning, after Cary phoned. Thought I ought to put something on for him. You know how sociable these Americans are. And you'll make all the difference to his enjoyment."

"You're too modest. You know he regards you with awe and reverence, a shining star in his firmament."

"Nonsense," said Conrad, smiling. "Come for my sake, then. Help me do the honours. I need my treasured assistant on such occasions."

"Flattery," she replied, shaking her head. "All right. Just for an hour or so, but I may be a little late. Would you like me to post that letter for you?"

"Thank you, my dear. It would save me a walk. Didn't seem worth getting the car out, but I'm not an enthusiastic walker, as you know. Until this evening, then. Bless you."

She posted the letter at the end of the lane and drove slowly home, for once not relishing the party ahead. Cary Pearston, she recalled, was the young American whose attitude to Conrad had been not dissimilar to Barry's attitude to the county cricket captain. He had met Conrad in his student days when the latter had been on a lecture tour in America and had issued a casual invitation to the young man if he should ever be in England. . . The invitation had been taken up and he had stayed at Valery Mount for a week, during which Josephine, in her first year with Conrad, had been deputed to take him around, show him the English countryside and some stately homes. Conrad himself had been working on a novel and so it was Josephine who had taken the brunt, second-hand, of Cary's youthful hero-worship. And that had been one more piece of coal on the fire that was consuming her engagement to Mike. She sighed. Looking back, she had to admit that Mike had cause to complain, for Conrad had monopolised her then as he did now. What with trips abroad, and social commitments at home in the cause of publicity, as well as a full day's work, she must have been very poor value from Mike's point of view.

And there she was again, back at that old bone of contention. Bother Mike, she thought, exasperated at the way all roads seemed to lead her thoughts to him since that encounter at Guy and Sophie's house-warming. Her mind went back to that fine spring evening before Mike had reappeared in her life, when she had lingered on her way home in a blissful state of complacency about her life. There was no reason why she should not dismiss him from her mind and regain that confidence. No reason at all, she thought crossly as she pulled up outside her home with an uncharacteristic jerk and left the car outside in readiness for the party that evening for which she felt no enthusiasm whatever. A lot of empty talk and false bonhomie. Everybody paying court to Conrad. She was just not in the mood. She would sooner have had a quiet evening with some music.

# 5

# *No Way Back*

A few weeks later, Hester Northbridge gave a party in her flat to celebrate the publication of her tenth book and return hospitality due to her small circle of friends. Josephine accepted the invitation with a firm resolve to make a last effort to put her relationship with Mike on a socially acceptable footing.

The first evening suggested by Hester had to be changed, since Mike, she said, could not manage it, and she therefore put it forward a week. Mike trying to wriggle out of it to avoid seeing her, thought Josephine. But it was not easy to continue to wriggle out of it when you lived in the flat below. She dressed for the occasion as though going into battle. A silk jersey dress the colour of sherry. Gold chain and ear-rings. Brown patent court shoes. Too sophisticated for the occasion? Her dark brown eyes looked back at her doubtfully from the mirror. Then she braced herself. She needed all the armour she could muster to tackle Mike. She had spent several evenings with Hester since that encounter in the restaurant, and a warm friendship was growing between them which she would not allow Mike to hamper. If they couldn't be friends, she and Mike, then they must be able to meet without embarrassment.

They were eight in all. Jean and Darrel Brynton, Guy and Sophie, Mike and Nick Barbury, a writer whose work Josephine knew but whom she had never met. Just a nice number to fit round my dining-table, Hester had said.

When Josephine arrived, they were all there except Mike, who followed almost on her heels bearing a bottle cradled in each arm.

"To launch the new book," he said, kissing Hester, who was still holding Josephine's flowers in her arms.

"Champagne! My dear Mike! How generous and dear of you! You shall have the privilege of opening it for me."

The dining-table was laid at the back of the large room. A wide bay window looked out over the sea, and as the evening was warm, Hester had opened the doors on to the balcony and they sat out there chatting while Hester put the finishing touches to the meal. Josephine found herself next to the fair-haired, handsome Nick Barbury, and congratulated him on the success of his latest biography. He was a witty and easy companion, modest about his own work, a shade dry about Conrad's, generous about Hester's books.

"In the top flight of that genre. Well written, nice cool sense of humour, and characters that live and are not puppets to serve an ingenious plot of murder or mayhem. I've been a fan from early on."

And talking about literary matters to Nick Barbury as the sun began to sink behind the downs and the sea darkened under a pink-streaked sky put Josephine in a pleasantly relaxed mood, able to ignore Mike, who was at the other end of the balcony sitting next to Jean. He had greeted her politely and briefly, and then had put the greatest distance possible between them.

He stage-managed his position skilfully at the supper table, too, for when Hester indicated the chair next to Josephine for him, he said cheerfully,

"If you want me to dispense champagne, I'll need some elbow room. Can I have the other end of the table? Then the ice bucket can go on the floor beside me."

"Of course. Silly of me. Just swop with Guy, will you, Mike?"

Hester started them off with melon, followed this with a delicious casserole of chicken, then produced bowls of strawberries, cream, an assortment of cheese and crusty home-made bread.

"My one culinary speciality, good bread," she said, when congratulated on it. "I can't eat what passes for bread in this country, and don't see why I should inflict it on my friends."

As they laughed and argued and talked nineteen to the dozen, Josephine could not help comparing the easy informality and frankness of this party with the parties she attended for Conrad. These were smooth enough, but too smooth, too polished, with people to be cultivated, others to be treated warily. More like diplomatic receptions.

Darrel, a keen conservationist, led them all into battle on the pros and cons of this topic, he and his supporters having by far the best of the argument, for he was an experienced campaigner, and was skilfully supported by Mike. They ranged from the siting of nuclear power stations to motorways, until, the opposition demolished, Darrel said,

"And where do you stand on this, Josephine? You've been keeping very quiet."

"For the conservationists, but with reservations. I think there's a case for compromise."

"A very diplomatic answer," said Mike smoothly, and she could have hit him as she met his sardonic smile.

"Of course there's a case for compromise," said Nick, coming to her rescue, and they were at it again.

It was difficult to imagine a greater contrast in appearance and style than between Nick Barbury and Mike, thought Josephine, as Nick parried Mike's points with an urbane wit that kept the temperature down. Nick, fair-haired, slim, elegant, cool. Mike, rugged, strongly built, with a suggestion of smouldering passion in his dark face, for all his assured control. There were two sides to Mike's personality, she thought. Or two that she knew, for in many ways he seemed a stranger to her now. There was the keen, rational mind of the lawyer, impatient with muddled thinking, cutting right through sentiment to the facts. And there was the warm, volatile side, with passionately felt feelings and a low flash-point. He had lifted her to heights of enjoyment when she was young that she had never experienced with anybody else. His sheer vitality had fired her, too. And had made their few differences equally fierce, but never with any aftermath of resentment or bitternes, until that last year. Perhaps it was the Cornish blood of his father that explained the volatile side, and the English blood of his mother, whom Josephine only dimly remembered, that accounted for the cool legal mind. She wondered how he reconciled these two warring factions. The tanned boy with the unruly hair, dressed in navy blue sweater and trousers, handling the sailing dinghy on a holiday in Cornwall. She had been fifteen then. He had been staying with his grandmother, she had gone there with her parents for a fortnight's holiday. He loved the sea. Was at home with boats. His blue eyes the colour of the Cornish sea. And the dark-suited professional man, emotions battened down, single-minded, razor sharp mind. And now, the hostile stranger to her, with a bitterness she had never known in him before.

She sighed at the complexity of this man who never seemed to give her any peace these days, and sipped her champagne for reassurance. Once, when the conversation had shifted to books and writers, and Nick and Hester led the field, she looked up and caught Mike with his guard down, watching her with an expression that pierced her. She could hardly define it, but she knew that pain and incredulity and unhappiness were there. She remembered that same look in her mother's eyes after her father had died. A look that said, it's not true, it can't be. Then, so swiftly that she wondered afterwards if she had imagined it, the expression had changed to a cold dispassionate appraisal that made her flush and turn her attention elsewhere.

It was warm in the room in spite of the open doors to the balcony, and they took their coffee outside while Hester played a record of some Kurt Weil songs heavy with regret and a Chekov-like mood of nostalgia. It was very peaceful there, with the dark sea below, the distant lights round the bay, a starry moonless sky above. At regular intervals the beam from a lightship broke across the sea. The mood of the music sent Josephine's thoughts back to the poem about the paths of summer. She and Mike had walked those paths once, when life had been simple and a warm affection between them had made their steps light. It had come to an end. She had brought it to an end. But he had made no attempt to build a bridge over the break made by their anger at that last meeting when both of them had said things in hot blood which afterwards he might have regretted, as she had. So why the bitterness now? The barely masked hatred?

Although the party had taken on a reflective, peaceful mood under the influence of the calm night and the broody music, there was no peace in Josephine's mind. She felt edgy, conscious all the time of Mike's presence, uneasy at the recollection of that disturbing moment when his mask had slipped. Remembering his kindness to Barry, she felt that the old Mike was still there underneath the spiked barrier he put up against her. She would make one more effort to reach him, to try to turn the enmity into at least a neutral acceptance of her presence among their friends. Since he so skilfully kept his distance, this was not easy. She lingered behind until she and Mike were the last guests, but he showed no disposition to depart, and Josephine left him ruminating on the balcony when she said goodbye to Hester. His flat was immediately beneath Hester's. She had visited it when Guy and Sophie lived there. She waited now just inside the alcove of his door. He came running down the stairs within five minutes, then froze as he saw her.

"I want to talk to you, Mike. Can I come in for a few minutes?"

"No. You and I have nothing to say to each other, Josephine."

"But I have. We can't go on being enemies like this."

"Why not? Enemies, in any case, isn't the right word."

She ignored any niceties of terminology and said quietly,

"Because we have mutual friends. I want to enjoy their company. I can't if I feel your hostility like a hidden bomb on the premises."

"Dear me, that's too bad. I should hate you to feel uncomfortable. In view of the past, that really is comic."

"Please let me in for a few minutes. We can't talk here. It's nearly midnight and we could disturb your neighbours."

"Not to worry. Nobody within earshot, and in any case

I'm not stopping to talk. These past years have certainly given you a cool nerve. When you smash up someone's house, you don't say afterwards 'It makes me feel uncomfortable when you don't seem friendly.' At least, you don't unless you have a very exalted idea about other people's duty to make you feel comfortable."

"But need there be this bitterness?" she asked angrily.

"Listen, Josephine." He spoke with a quiet intensity that chilled her. "I hoped never to see you again. I wouldn't have accepted this partnership with Guy if I'd known you were acquainted with him and that we might meet. I thought this was far enough away from Elmfield to run no risk of chance encounters. Unfortunately, I was wrong. But I want nothing whatever to do with you again. You've done enough damage, and if you'd a shred of sensibility, you'd keep your distance from me. That's final. Do you understand?"

"Yes," she said cuttingly. "I never knew that pride could distort a man's nature so disastrously."

He lifted his eyes heavenwards and raised his arms, both fists clenched, as though hardly able to contain himself, then said savagely,

"Keep out of my way, Josephine. That's all. Keep out of my way."

He unlocked his door and closed it with a slam in her face. She leaned against the wall of the alcove, trembling and shocked at the intensity of his hostility. Then she pulled herself together and went down the stairs and out into the warm night air. She sat in her car for several minutes, fighting to regain her composure before she started the drive home. That was the end, she thought. She was well rid of a man so eaten up with pride, so full of resentment after four years, that he could not spare a civil word for a girl who had had the temerity to break off an engagement after a quarrel in which he had been quite brutal. His nature had changed completely, or else she had never known the real Mike Wexford. The paths of summer. They seemed now like an old dream, an illusion. And yet they had been real, a long time ago. But there was no way back. No way at all, she thought as she pressed the starter and moved off on her lonely drive home.

# 6
# A Campaign of Gossip

July came and went with a spell of sultry weather and scattered thunder-storms which did not help Conrad's unusually nervy state about his play, now running into casting difficulties.

"I don't find this producer sympathetic," he said. "He doesn't really understand my characters. And he will keep trying to re-write bits of it."

He was in London a great deal, and for once Josephine found herself with time on her hands during his absence. In August the play went into rehearsal and at the end of the month Conrad had a final row with the producer and walked out, declaring that he would take no further part, would leave it to the producer and if it flopped, he, for one, wouldn't be surprised, since in his opinion it had been emasculated.

After a somewhat trying day, soothing Conrad's ruffled feelings and coping with a V.A.T. inspector and the accountant who looked after Conrad's tax matters, Josephine walked home slowly, welcoming the calm of the evening. Hawthorn berries were showing red in the hedgerows, the first tints of autumn were appearing on birch trees and brambles, and a robin sang its plaintive little song as she came to the village green. As she was passing the general store, an elderly woman came hurrying out, head bent as she stowed her purchases into a bag, and almost collided with her. She began to apologise.

"I do beg your pardon, I wasn't looking..." Her

tentative little smile faded and her pleasant face hardened as she recognised Josephine.

"Why, it's Mrs. Waycross," said Josephine with a warm smile, for she had always liked this buxom little woman who had been Dr. Wexford's housekeeper ever since Mike's mother had died, and had become a much-loved member of the household over the years.

"Good evening, Josephine," she said stiffly.

"It's some years since I last saw you, but you look just the same. You left the village when Dr. Wexford retired, didn't you?"

"I did," she said grimly.

Puzzled by her stiff manner, for she had always been a kindly, cheerful person, Josephine said,

"Where do you live now? Far away?"

"With my sister in Westbrook. I came in on the bus to see an old friend."

"I expect you were sorry to leave Dr. Wexford and Elmfield, after all those years."

At these words, Mrs. Waycross drew herself up like a pugnacious duck protecting her young, her round cheeks flushed, her eyes bright.

"That I was. But it was even worse for the doctor and Mike, driven out by those malicious tongues, inspired by you, more shame to you. I'll say it, if nobody else will. And now I'll bid you good evening."

Josephine caught her arm as she turned to go.

"Please explain, Mrs. Waycross. I don't know what you're talking about. What malicious tongues?"

"You ask that? All those people you told lies to about Mike, and a nicer, kinder young man never breathed. A bit spirited, maybe, but a fine young man, as you well knew until you grew tired of him and wanted him out of

61

your way, never mind how much you hurt other people as well as Mike. The doctor never wanted to leave Elmfield when he retired. Not after all those years. And nor did I want to lose the job that had been more than a job to me. You ought to be ashamed of yourself, my girl, for what you did. I would never have believed it of you. You, such a nice girl, we all thought, the daughter of the doctor's old friend. But I can see it doesn't trouble your conscience at all. I'm sorry to have to speak out like this, but coming here today and seeing the old place brought it all back. And then meeting you, so smiling and uncaring. I shan't come back here again, to be reminded of such things."

She turned away, trying to mask her emotions. Josephine caught her arm again.

"Please, Mrs. Waycross, tell me what happened. I honestly don't know. I was abroad for six months when this took place. When I got back, Dr. Wexford had retired and gone to live with his sister in Cornwall. That was all I knew."

"You'd laid the foundations before you went, then. Ask that housekeeper at Valery Mount. She did your work well for you. I've nothing more to say to you," she concluded, pulling her arm free and walking across the green towards the bus stop.

Bewildered and troubled, Josephine walked on slowly, almost colliding with a cyclist as she crossed the lane to climb the footpath up the hill, unseeing, going over in her mind every word that Mrs. Waycross had uttered.

In the garden, she found her mother dead-heading the dahlias.

"Hullo, darling. You look tired. What's the matter?" she added as she met Josephine's eyes.

"I met Mrs. Waycross in the village. You remember. Dr. Wexford's housekeeper."

"Of course. A dear soul. Devoted to Doc and Mike. Went to live with her sister, I believe."

"Yes. She was visiting a friend here today. She told me I was to blame for Dr. Wexford leaving here when he retired. Blamed me, too, for what I did to Mike by causing malicious gossip. Do you know anything about it, Mother? Do you recollect any gossip?"

Her mother looked astonished.

"Gossip? What kind of gossip?"

"I don't know. I'd no idea what she was talking about."

"Nor I. Oh, I expect she was sorry you broke off your engagement. Saw it as a slur on her beloved family."

"No, it was more than that," said Josephine slowly. "She said that Conrad's housekeeper was at the centre of it, at my instigation."

"Well, I heard no talk. No criticism of you. Why should I? A broken engagement is a private affair."

"But you don't mingle with the people down in the village. You've never been a mixer."

"True. I've too much to interest me here. Don't worry about it now, dear. I expect Mrs. Waycross is making too much of it because she was unhappy at losing her job. Whatever happened is over and done with a long time ago."

"But it isn't. That's the trouble. It isn't over for Mrs. Waycross. And it isn't over for Mike. It lives on. That bitter core of resentment. I'm going to get to the bottom of it."

"Why, dear? What good can it do, digging it up now? That is, if there's anything to dig up except a little gossip, which is no unusual thing in any small community."

63

"I need to know. Ever since meeting Mike again, I've felt that something was wrong. Over and above the natural awkwardness and unhappy reminders that might have been expected. I don't like mysteries. I'm going to get to the bottom of this one, since it concerns people I was fond of, and still am."

"How will you start?" asked her mother, recognising from the set of Josephine's jaw that she would not be deterred.

"I had thought I'd start with Mrs. Midhurst, but I shan't get much change out of her, I'm pretty sure. A more buttoned-up character I've never come across. I can come back to her later. I think I shall try Dr. Wexford first. He was fond of me and we always got on well. He'll tell me the truth, I'm sure."

"Will you write to him? I don't know his address."

"No, I shall go and see him. This isn't something that can be settled by correspondence. I'll see if I can get his address from the people who bought his house."

"It certainly was odd, the way Doc went without saying goodbye to me. He was such a good friend to David, and so kind to me when David died. I should have tried to get in touch myself. I'm well aware of my sins of omission where human relationships are concerned. They have never mattered to me a great deal because I had David, and you."

"Well, why should you worry if your world was complete?"

"You would. You have a much more outgoing nature than I, dear. People matter to you. But . . . you and Mike. I wonder whether any good will come of delving into the past."

"I want to understand what happened to Mike, Mother. He's so bitter."

"You want him back?"

"No, no. Nothing like that. Mike's changed. I've changed. We're two different people now. We can never meet on that old footing again. But I can't bear to feel that I'm an object of hatred to him, without knowing why. I shall ask Conrad for some leave, and go to Cornwall."

"Well, you're certainly due for some leave. You haven't had a proper holiday on your own since you joined him."

"The trips abroad have made holidays seem redundant, somehow. I have let him take over my life, though, haven't I?" she added thoughtfully.

"Yes, but you've enjoyed doing so. He is, after all, a famous man. He's proved a fine education for you. Brought you out. You needed to have your horizons widened. We lead such a quiet, cloistered life here."

"No need to sound guilty about that. I like my home. Always have. And if that sounds unusual these days, you can take the credit for it. There's a large earwig emerging from that red dahlia."

"Dahlias and earwigs go together like fish and chips. It's time I stopped. Good heavens!" she added as she glanced at her watch. "It's long past the time when I should have stopped. I've a casserole in the oven that's probably gone dry."

"It smelt good when I came through the kitchen."

"Just take those to the compost heap, will you, dear?" called her mother over her shoulder as she hurried back to the house.

Josephine trundled the wheelbarrow full of half faded dahlia flowers to the heap at the end of the garden. They made a rich tapestry of colour. The garden glowed with colour at that season of the year, but she saw nothing of the sunflowers and michaelmas daisies and fuchsias, did not notice the red admiral and peacock butterflies on the red sedum, only saw the anger and distress on Mrs. Waycross's round flushed face.

The next morning, on her way to work, she called at the house where the Wexfords had lived, once as familiar to her as her own. The present owner, a pleasant-faced, elderly woman, could not remember Dr. Wexford's present address.

"He left a change-of-address card with us in case there was anything to be forwarded, and we kept it for a few months, but we haven't got it now and I can't remember it. I do remember the village, though, because we'd stayed there once on holiday. Mawnsey. It's only a small fishing village, and I'm sure a letter would get to him if you just addressed it to Dr. Wexford at Mawnsey, North Cornwall."

Josephine thanked her and went on her way. That morning, she asked Conrad for a week's leave. He looked surprised but agreed at once.

"Of course, my dear. As long as you're back for the first night of the play. You won't want to miss that, I'm sure. You put a lot of work into the research. Afraid our efforts have been largely nullified by the mauling hands of our producer, but I must have you with me to sustain me on the night. I'm not optimistic."

"I'll be there."

"Where are you going?"

"To Cornwall. I've an old friend there I'd like to look up."

"A break will do you good. Could do with one myself. May slip away to the Dordogne. Have a few days with Lance and Polly. Otherwise I know Brian's going to nag me about my novel. We'll get down to that after the play's launched. Go to Switzerland and work there for a month or two, perhaps. I always work well there. The air invigorates me. Nice change for you, too."

\*     \*     \*

Josephine took two days for her drive to Cornwall, stopping at a hotel in the New Forest for the first night. She reached Mawnsey in the late afternoon of the next day. It was tucked away at the foot of a narrow twisting road to the sea, a scatter of cottages and houses grouped round the bay, with high cliffs at each end. A few shops, a small inn. No hotel. It was only a few miles from Lenstow, the seaside town where Mike's grandmother had lived and she had spent that long-ago holiday with her parents, and she decided to return there to seek accommodation. It was far more crowded there than she remembered, but she managed to find a room in a small hotel at the back of the town.

The next morning, she consulted the local telephone directory and found a Miss Muriel Wexford living at Mawnsey. When she telephoned, it was Dr. Wexford himself who answered. She found herself trembling a little as she announced herself, and the only response was a long pause. Then the doctor's voice came, formal and chilly.

"Josephine Riverton. Well, this *is* a surprise. Why are you phoning me?"

"Because I want to see you. May I come over this morning?"

"I hardly think there's anything we could possibly have to discuss."

"It is important. I shouldn't have driven all the way

67

from Sussex if it weren't. Will you please give me just half an hour of your time this morning? Please."

There was another pause. Then,

"Very well. I shall be here until eleven. Tamarisk Cottage is at the end of Cobb Lane."

He rang off and left her wincing at the change from the gruff but kindly manner of the doctor she had known from childhood. It was not going to be a very happy visit, she thought.

Tamarisk Cottage was long and low, sturdily built in the granite stone of most of the village, and well sited at the end of a lane near the bottom of the hill down to the sea. The door was opened by Dr. Wexford. Tall and strongly built, like Mike, he stooped more than she remembered and his face was more lined, but he looked tanned and fit as he stood there regarding her gravely.

"Come in, Josephine."

He led her to a pleasant sitting-room, furnished with comfortable armchairs, lots of cushions, gleaming brass. A spaniel was drowsing in a patch of sun by the window and took no notice of the new arrival beyond lifting its head, giving a small wag with its stump of a tail, and dropping its head down again.

"My sister is away for the week," he said, indicating an armchair. "What is your business?"

She plunged straight in.

"I met Mrs. Waycross, your old housekeeper, in the village last week and learned for the first time that there had been gossip about Mike and me after our engagement was broken off. I was in Switzerland then for six months, and knew nothing of any gossip, nor did I hear any when I got back. Will you please tell me what it was about."

"You should know," he said drily.

"But that's the point," she cried. "I don't. All I know is that after a series of quarrels with Mike over my job, which he resented, we had a terrible row in which we both said things that I, for one, regretted afterwards, and I gave him back his engagement ring and said it was all over. A few days later, I went abroad. When I came back, you and Mike had both disappeared from the scene. That is all I know."

"What is the point of bringing it up now? The damage was done. It can't be righted."

"But what damage? I ought to know, since I'm the one blamed. I caused Mike great unhappiness by breaking our engagement. I caused myself unhappiness too. But I had the right to change my mind when things were going so badly. I was sorry. But was that a crime? Because I don't know of any other. I know nothing of any malicious gossip."

"Perhaps not, since you went away. But you must have provided the material for it."

"Let's not go into the rights and wrongs of it. Tell me what it was. Tell me what happened while I was away. Because I don't know," she said, beating her fist on her knee in desperate emphasis.

Dr. Wexford leaned back in his chair, his elbows on the arms, hands clasped, studying her. Then he said in a measured voice,

"Very well. It's not something I'm happy to recollect, but since you ask, I'll spell it out. You may not have meant to do so much damage. I don't know. I learned afterwards that the chief broadcaster of my son's unstable and violent character was Conrad Ravensburg's housekeeper. I don't know when the gossip started, but it was a week or two after your engagement came to an end that it began to

69

reach me. Mrs. Waycross had taken the brunt of it before then, as she explained when, after a patient of mine had passed some odd remarks about Mike, I asked her if she knew anything about it. It was all over the village, I learned, that Ravensburg had removed you for your own safety to work in Switzerland for a while, since you were on the verge of a nervous breakdown caused by harassment and brutality from Mike because you had broken off the engagement."

Josephine stared at him.

"That's crazy."

"I laughed it off at first, and said nothing to Mike. It was just ridiculous gossip. Had I thought of getting Mike to see a psychiatrist? That was one kind lady's remark. I took little notice, but the talk persisted. I still said nothing about it to Mike, but the boy was beginning to look strained and I guessed it was reaching him. Then he came home one day in a state of fury that might have justified the gossip," said Dr. Wexford drily. "He asked me if I'd heard any talk about him, and when I said I had, he threw a copy of a letter on the table. Ravensburg had written it from Switzerland to Mr. Ennerdale, the senior partner of Mike's firm. He knew him because they'd both served on a fund-raising committee for some charity. We presumed he wrote it at your instigation."

"This gets crazier and crazier. I knew nothing about any letter. I never discussed Mike with Conrad. Never."

"Then why should he write it?"

"What did he say?"

Dr. Wexford regarded her steadily for a moment or two. He doesn't believe me, she thought. Then he said,

"I may still have a copy of it. Ennerdale refused to let Mike keep the original, but left it with him that morning to reflect on, and Mike took a photo-copy, with some wild idea of suing Ravensburg for libel. When he calmed down, of course, he realised that the publicity would damage all of us and that it wouldn't compensate him for your betrayal, anyway. He told me to burn it. I kept it, because I'd no mind to let Ravensburg get away with it without tackling him and you about it. But in the end, I did nothing. Once gossip of this sort starts, you can't stop it. Can only let it die down for lack of fuel."

"Will you see if you can find it and show it to me?"

"Very well," he said, shrugging, and left her. He was gone for about ten minutes, and Josephine paced up and down the room, bewildered and horrified at Dr. Wexford's disclosures.

"Here it is," he said. "I meant to destroy it when I moved but it stayed among some papers in my desk which I hadn't bothered to sort out."

She walked to the window and read it.


My dear Ennerdale,

Since we have collaborated so happily on the committee and I have formed a high opinion of your tact, I am taking the liberty of approaching you on a somewhat delicate matter.

My young secretary has been brought to a state of nervous exhaustion and fear by the behaviour of one of your employees, Mike Wexford, to whom she was engaged. For very good reasons, she has broken off the engagement, but his violent threats and constant harassment have brought her to such a state that I felt compelled to do something about it. She is only twenty, has led a sheltered life and recently lost her father, so I feel some responsibility for her health and security.

71

You may wonder what this has to do with you, but I feel that you might be able to bring some influence to bear on the young man. These passionate obsessions can be dangerous, but perhaps a few wise words of counsel from you would have effect. Such uncontrolled conduct is, after all, hardly what one expects from a member of your profession, and there is always the possibility of adverse publicity arising in the future if police protection had to be sought in the case of threatened violence. Only a remote possibility, I'm sure, and I am hopeful that a period of six months abroad for my secretary and a few words of counsel for the young man from you might bring this unhappy situation to an end. We live in such undisciplined days that I think it wiser to try to forestall serious trouble if at all possible, which is why I hope you will forgive me troubling you.

Your sterling co-operation on the committee was greatly appreciated. That we reached our target was due in no small measure to your efforts. Committees, alas, do so often attract well-meaning but woolly-minded members. Your decisiveness and clarity of thought were of the utmost value.

Yours sincerely

Conrad Ravensburg

Josephine looked up, speechless, then read it again. "I can't believe it," she said. "I can't believe it. Why should he write like this?"

"To protect you, apparently," said Dr. Wexford drily.

"From Mike? The boy I'd known all my life? My friend? And he was still that, right to the end."

"Whatever you thought about Mike, that was the impression you must have given Ravensburg."

"No. He's not a fool. He doesn't get crazily wrong impressions like that. I never once discussed Mike with Conrad. He knew we were engaged, and he met Mike once, when he opened the garden for charity and Mike came. I was serving teas. I'd had to cancel an outing we'd planned because Conrad called me in to take over the teas when the housekeeper went down with a migraine, so Mike wasn't in a very affable mood. We had a quarrel and Conrad overheard a somewhat angry parting between us that afternoon. He passed some quizzical remark. I don't remember now what it was." She spoke slowly, thinking back, trying to make sense of Conrad's action.

"You must have given him the impression at the end that you felt threatened."

"No, never. The only other time I mentioned Mike was when Conrad noticed that my engagement ring had vanished and he asked me whether it was over between Mike and me. I said yes, it just hadn't worked out. Then he said that perhaps it was a good thing he'd decided to work in Switzerland for the next few months. It would take my mind off it. And that," she concluded, "was all that ever passed between Conrad and me about Mike. He did ask me recently whether I'd ever seen him again and I said no. That's the sum total of it."

"Did you act in a distraught manner at the time?"

"No. I'm not the distraught type. I was angry with Mike, and unhappy about it all, but I was my normal self as far as my job with Conrad was concerned. I was surprised and sorry that both you and Mike had left Elmfield when I got home, without a word to my mother or me. I understand now. No wonder Mike is so bitter. He left his job because of that letter?"

"Yes. He couldn't bear to think that his most private

and personal affairs were being discussed in that way. He never liked Ennerdale much, anyway. A social climber. He would be very flattered by the attention of the Great Man. The job in London offered Mike far more scope. But most of all, he wanted to get away from Elmfield, from the curious looks and whispering tongues, from memories of you. He loved you, Josephine. And hurt from those you love goes in very deeply."

She sat down, clasping her head between her hands, her voice muffled.

"I wouldn't have had it happen like that for the world. Not to do that to Mike and you. Was that why you left Elmfield, too?"

"Yes. I knew Mike would never want to come back to see me there after he'd got to London. And I was sickened by the whole affair. My sister had long wanted me to join her here when I retired. Our roots are here. It's a long way for Mike to come. I miss him, of course, but he comes down when he has time, and I've quite taken to life here now."

Josephine looked up as a new thought struck her. "Why didn't I hear anything about it after I got home? Six months isn't so very long."

"Mrs. Waycross said that Ravensburg's housekeeper had put it about that it would be kind not to mention the subject again after your return. That you had recovered, but wanted no reminders. Poor Mrs. Waycross. She was eager to make that point clear, that there would be no more talk, hoping it would persuade me to stay, because she was very attached to us. But I couldn't. It had all gone sour on me. I was very fond of you, too, Josephine, and of your mother. It was hard to take."

"Can't you believe me when I say that I'm in no way to

blame for that slanderous talk? I never felt any ill feeling towards Mike. Never. I just wanted to be free to enjoy my new job. I would have preferred to stay friends. I hoped we would. Why should I want to harry him like that?"

"To be rid of a rather persistent man who might hamper your new found freedom. Mike doesn't give up easily."

"How could he think I'd stoop to that? How could he or you think it of me?"

"My dear, I'm getting old. I find the young generation hard to understand these days. Mike thought that Ravensburg had quite taken you over. That you were under his spell. That was the only excuse he could find. And, after all, what else could we believe? Why should your employer act as he did unless on your behalf, in answer to your appeal?"

"I don't know why, but I shall find out. I know I'm useful to him and that he might not welcome a marriage which might take me away from him. Which *would* take me away, because that job allows me little personal life of my own. But to go to such lengths? It's hard to believe. No, there must be some reason for Conrad having misread the situation. But I intend to get to the bottom of it."

"Is there much point in raking it all up again now?"

"Of course there is. You know how bitter and jaundiced Mike is. If I can get the truth through to him, some, at least, of that bitterness could be removed."

"Do you still care, Jo?"

At least the use of the name he had always called her by indicated a certain softening on his part, she thought, as she said slowly,

"I care that Mike should be so embittered. It could sour

75

his whole life. But we're strangers now. Foolish to think we could ever go back. We start from now. But he won't let me get within miles of him, so how I'm to get the truth to him I don't know, but somehow I'm going to, once I've found out exactly who started that campaign and why. Can't *you* believe me? That would help."

He spoke slowly, measuring his words.

"Yes, perhaps I can go along with you most of the way, because I knew your parents so well and I've great faith in genetic heredity. I always thought you took after your father. He was a man of complete integrity. But I must say I can't see any motive for an outsider attacking Mike like that. Not that people need much encouragement to gossip, and any crumb that drops from Ravensburg's table is snapped up by the locals."

"You share Mike's dislike of him?"

"I hardly know him well enough to judge, but he strikes me as a vain man, the complete egoist, and I never have much cared for people who nurture an image for public consumption."

No, thought Josephine, the doctor was certainly not a man to subscribe to image-making. His brusque, blunt approach to his patients had made no concessions to a soothing bedside manner, which had probably rebounded on him when gossip had presented some of the hypo-chondriacs in his care with a weapon to get back at him.

"Well," she said, standing up, "thank you for seeing me. It's not much good saying I'm sorry, is it, with the damage done? But I am. Deeply. I shan't rest until I've got to the bottom of it and tried to repair a little of the damage to Mike."

"My dear," he said, taking her hand, his eyes kinder

76

now, "take care how you handle him. He'll be hard to convince, and he could hurt you."

"Not as much as I've hurt him. And I'm not afraid of Mike, you know. It's just a case of getting him to unlock the door if I think I've a case to put to him."

"Well, if I can help in any way, let me know. Whether you're wise to dig it up after all these years is hard to say. Remember me kindly to your mother. Did she not mention the gossip to you when you got home?"

"No. It all passed over Mother's head. She has a world of her own, you know. The garden. She has very little to do with the local community."

"Perhaps she's wise. A private world of one's own is very welcome when you reach our age. I've taken up painting myself. Had a studio built in the garden. Not much good at it, but I enjoy it. Where are you staying?"

"In Lenstow. I shall rest tomorrow, then drive back to start investigations. I hardly recognised Lenstow. Remember that holiday we all spent there, years ago?"

"When my mother was alive. A lot has changed since then, my dear. It's a good rule never to go back."

She smiled and left him. Driving back to Lenstow, she felt a little comforted by his friendlier attitude, but aghast at the ugly scenario of her break with Mike, aware of a deep sense of loss which she could never make good, however much she tried. But she was going to try, nevertheless.

# 7

# The Housekeeper's View

Josephine decided to say nothing to Conrad until she had made further investigations. Two days after her return, she accompanied him to the first night of his play, which was politely if not enthusiastically received. Several friends shared their box, feeding Conrad with compliments during the evening, clapping madly when he appeared with the cast and producer on stage before the final curtain. Josephine felt herself curiously detached from the proceedings. The play seemed to lack conviction, and although she agreed with Conrad that the producer had not improved it by his changes, she doubted whether it would have stood up any better in its original form.

Conrad gave a supper party afterwards which went on too long for her, and she was glad when she was finally alone in the bedroom of the hotel where she and Conrad always stayed when he was in London and needed her there, too. Looking at herself in the mirror, she seemed unreal, too. That young woman in the midnight blue chiffon dress and silver drop ear-rings which matched the silver chain round her neck, what had she to do with Jo Riverton? She had watched Conrad that evening as though he was a stranger, too. A handsome man of great charm surrounded by a shoal of admiring friends like those little fishes that swam in the wake of whales. The girl in the mirror was one of those little fishes, too. How important a little fish had she been to Conrad to make him want to keep her in his wake?

They returned to Elmfield the next day, Conrad in a restrained mood after reading the luke-warm reviews in the papers. After he had settled some income tax problems with his accountant and the inspector of taxes, he would make plans to spend the next few months in Switzerland, working on his new novel, he said. The prospect, however, did not seem to arouse in him a great deal of enthusiasm.

That evening, when she left the office, she sought out Mrs. Midhurst, who looked surprised when she saw Josephine at the door of the flat.

"I'm sorry to trouble you, Mrs. Midhurst, but I wonder if you could spare me a few minutes?"

"Of course. Come in. I'm ironing. You won't mind if I carry on?"

Josephine followed her through the little hall into the kitchen. It was a bright room, scrupulously clean and tidy, with white walls above pale blue tiles which matched the blue and white floor covering. Mrs. Midhurst picked up Barry's shirt from a pile of clothes waiting to be ironed and said,

"What can I do for you, Miss Riverton? Is Barry causing any trouble?"

"No. He never does. This concerns me. I've only recently learned that four years ago, while I was away with Mr. Ravensburg in Switzerland, a lot of talk went on in the village about my engagement to Mike Wexford. I was told it originated from you. I expect you remember what it was about,"

"Certainly. An unhappy business, but, thanks to Mr. Ravensburg, you had no more trouble, I believe."

"It was Mr. Ravensburg who instructed you, then?"

"Of course."

"Didn't it occur to you that I should have been the person to consult first?"

Mrs. Midhurst looked astonished.

"You were in too distressed a state to be able to handle it, he said. It was lucky for you that you had an employer like Mr. Ravensburg to take up the cudgels on your behalf. I wish I'd had a helper like that when I was a girl. Men are such scoundrels," she added bitterly, "and women such dupes."

"But I didn't need Mr. Ravensburg's help, and Mike Wexford was no scoundrel. I wanted to break off my engagement because I preferred my job to marriage, and there was no combining the two. I did break it off, but I was never threatened in the way this gossip suggested. Mike Wexford, and his father, had been my friends for years. It wasn't exactly a happy time when I broke off the engagement, but to suggest that Mike was reducing me to a mental wreck, terrifying me by his brutal harassment, was absurd."

"Well, that was not the impression that Mr. Ravensburg had. He was very worried. He asked me to co-operate in making the truth known in the village in the hope that it would shame the young man into mending his ways and leaving you alone. I agreed willingly. I've been at the receiving end of men's violent, callous behaviour. I was only too glad to help to put one in his place. Why are you bothering about it now? He gave you no more trouble. Left the village. You should be grateful to Mr. Ravensburg. I would have been."

"It unjustly blackened the character of someone I'd known all my life, someone I was fond of even if I didn't want to marry him."

"I shouldn't worry about that overmuch. In my ex-

80

perience, men are not sensitive creatures. I really don't know what you're bothered about, Miss Riverton. You were helped to get rid of a man you didn't want, who was no good to you. You were lucky, I'd say," she said briskly, applying the iron with vigour to a blue table-cloth.

She was obviously going to get no further with this conversation, thought Josephine. Mrs. Midhurst's opinion of men justified any means to put them down.

"You never thought to check the truth of this gossip you were asked to spread?"

"Certainly not. Why should I doubt Mr. Ravensburg's word? Nor was it idle gossip. It was done to protect you, and, mistaken or not, I'm sure it was very kind of Mr. Ravensburg."

"I understand. I won't take up any more of your time."

Hilda Midhurst's pale blue eyes surveyed her calmly.

"Be thankful someone cared enough to take trouble to help you. I've not found many would do as much."

Josephine walked slowly across the garden, reflecting on what she had learned. So it was a calculated campaign, carried out behind her back, neatly planned to run its course and be concluded before she arrived back from Switzerland.

"Careful there," said a cheerful voice, as she stumbled over a garden rake.

Bill Mendon grinned up from the bed of geraniums he was weeding. He was a small, wiry man, with twinkling light grey eyes and a complexion like a russet apple. He talked with the flattened vowels of a Yorkshireman, and she had never known him other than good humoured. Difficult to judge his age, but she guessed him to be about forty, for he was lithe and active, and his black hair showed no hint of grey.

81

"Sorry, Bill. You've taken on a new hand, I see," she added as Barry staggered round the corner of the greenhouse bearing a pail, put it down and started crawling along a low hedge.

"Snail hunting. Had a plague of them this summer. Caused no end of damage. Barry looks for the silver trails and tries to track them down. Very keen, he is."

"I can imagine. How's the cricket coaching going?"

"If enthusiasm and perseverance could make a cricketer, young Barry would finish up in the English test team. Not a natural, though. I've persuaded his mum to let me take him to Lord's next Saturday. Pray for fine weather."

"I will. It's good of you to spare him so much of your time."

He sat back on his heels, looking across at Barry, whose curly head shone like brass in the early evening sun.

"Oh, I don't know. I'm fond of the kid. Doesn't have much of a life, I guess. Lonely. And the summer holiday's too long. We get on all right."

She smiled and walked on, glancing with a shudder into Barry's pail where several dead snails were gathered.

"Nine," he announced, emerging from the undergrowth with another victim to add to his bucket. "Salt water," he added for Josephine's edification. "It kills them right away."

She left him to it. That evening, over coffee, she told her mother what had transpired between herself and Mrs. Midhurst.

"It was obviously a deliberate campaign," she concluded.

"I can't believe it," said her mother. "Are you sure you didn't give him the wrong impression, Jo, in the distress of the moment?"

"Quite sure," said Josephine firmly.

"Then why?"

"Because he wanted to make sure I'd not be leaving him to get married. He wanted my services, permanently, and full time. There could be no other reason. But to spread such wicked talk, and even to write to Mike's employer, without a word to me, was iniquitous."

"It's been a shock to you. You've always thought so much of Conrad Ravensburg."

"You might say he'd taken me over. I admired him tremendously. And I've always felt grateful for his appreciation. Lapped up the flattery. And I've enjoyed the work, until now. How could Conrad go behind my back like that?"

"Perhaps he really did believe he was protecting you, dear. You were very young, after all."

"He had no grounds for believing I was in need of protection. No, Mother. I think it was solely for Conrad Ravensburg's benefit that he went to that trouble, quite unconcerned with any unhappiness he caused to Mike and his father. That's how I read it, but I shall have a word with Brian Renfrow tomorrow. He's coming to see Conrad, whom he's known for more than thirty years. I can confide in him. We're good friends, and he can tell me whether I'm being unjust to Conrad or not."

"And then?"

"I shall tackle Conrad. It won't be any good, of course. He'll have no difficulty in justifying himself, painting a noble picture. But I shall have my say. Nobody is going to run my life for me, and injure my friends at the same time," she concluded angrily, her eyes bright.

"And Mike?" asked her mother quietly. "Are you going to try to mend matters there?"

"I shall try to get the truth through to him, if I can ever get near enough. But whether he'll believe me... I've no proof, have I?"

"Dr. Wexford believed you."

"He didn't get the stab in the back. You wouldn't believe how much Mike has changed. He can't stand the sight of me now."

"You look tired to death, dear. Don't tear yourself to shreds over something that happened four years ago and can't be undone. It will do no good to upset Mr. Ravensburg and spoil a job you enjoy."

Josephine stared at her mother.

"You're under the spell of the Great Man, too. He mustn't be upset. I'm lucky to be able to bask in his reflected glory. Ought to be happy to be treated like a puppet. Is that it?"

"Don't look so fierce, darling. Your father was the same when he was roused, but don't act impulsively. I'm only saying that it's late in the day to try to mend matters."

"It's never too late to try to mend hurts to your friends," said Josephine more quietly.

"I stand rebuked. I do hate seeing you so distressed, though."

"I've been the one living in a cosy world of ignorance. I can't settle to anything this evening. I shall go for a walk over the downs. It's a beautiful evening. May calm me down."

When Josephine left the cottage, Joyce Riverton stood at the window with a troubled face and watched her daughter walking down the lane towards the downs. This whole business had come as a nasty shock to Jo. Conrad Ravensburg fallen from the high esteem in which she had always held him. Mike Wexford grievously damaged by her, although unwittingly. She sighed. Just as Jo's life had seemed so happy and settled. She hoped her daughter would not over-react. After all, it was old history. But Jo took after her father in her fierce hatred of injustice, and she would not rest until she had put it right, at no matter what cost to herself. She was an idealist, like her father, and compromise played no part in her life. And that, as Joyce Riverton knew only too well, was a bruising recipe for living.

# 8
# *Redress*

Brian Renfrow was closeted with Conrad all the next morning, and stayed to lunch, which Mrs. Midhurst served in the dining-room. She was an excellent cook, but was seldom called on during the day for anything more than a light lunch for Conrad on a tray, since Josephine chose to lunch at the little café in the village. Only for the occasional business visitor was a formal lunch laid on, for Conrad preferred to entertain in the evenings and was a frugal eater during the day. On these rare occasions, however, Josephine was expected to lunch with them, since she was *au fait* with all business matters. On that particular day, however, she found it difficult to keep her attention focused on details of negotiations, which had reached a critical stage, for the sale of valuable subsidiary rights in one of Conrad's early novels.

An opportunity to discuss her problem with Renfrow came after lunch when Conrad had an appointment with the inspector of taxes in Dilford, and she was left to finalise details of the deal. This done, she unburdened herself to him. He listened with his customary careful attention, and was silent for a few moments when she had told him the story, then said thoughtfully,

"That's the Conrad touch, I'm afraid. He can be as mischievous as a monkey to attain his ends. You'll never nail him, though. He may not be a good playwright, but he can write himself a good part and play it with great conviction."

"Doesn't it amaze you that he should go to such lengths? After all, I'd broken off the engagement in favour of my job. Where was the threat?"

"He wanted to make sure. You were young, could be persuaded to make it up again as long as young Wexford was in the vicinity. Would that have been out of the question?"

"I can't say. I didn't want to break off our friendship. I half hoped when I got back to restore a friendly footing. I'd known him for years. I was fond of him."

"Conrad sensed that. He's got sensitive feelers."

"It still seems outrageous to me."

Brian Renfrow leaned back in his chair and regarded her with shrewd, kind eyes.

"I don't think you've ever realised how valuable you are to Conrad. Not just as an efficient secretary, but as a literary aid. You can write well yourself. You're a splendid editor. How many of his articles have you written for him?"

"A good many. He gives me the material. They're his ideas. I merely write them up, and Conrad goes over them."

"Never failing to alter one or two little things?" suggested Renfrow with a twinkle in his eyes. "Just to salve his pride. Put his stamp on it."

"True."

"You've corrected his proofs, done most of any necessary research for him. And Conrad's beginning to run out of steam. You've been an invaluable prop. I'd say he'd stop at nothing to keep you."

"That's a bit disconcerting."

"You should be warned, though it's not in my interests to do so. I want to keep him working. In a way, I'm sorry for him. He dreads old age, must be aware himself that his literary capabilities are waning but doesn't seem to have acquired any philosophical approach to growing old. He can only pretend that it doesn't apply to him. And once he stops being in the literary swim, he could be very lonely. He'll find that large circle of friends and acquaintances will shrink very rapidly. He has no real capacity for making true friends, you know. He's a taker, not a giver."

"You're a real friend to him."

"He sees me as a well-meaning fusspot. Gets on better with my son these days. Well, I've decided to retire at the end of the year, and leave it to John. He'll be much better than I at helping Conrad to maintain his image without actually doing any worth-while work to justify it. John is a master at what I call the puff industry."

"I'm sorry you're retiring. You've done a lot for Conrad. I'm sure he appreciates it, deep down."

"Deep down in Conrad Ravensburg lives a man nobody knows, or is it just empty down there? I grow jaundiced. I shall hope to develop a more kindly nature when I devote my time to gardening. I've just bought a cottage in Dorset with a couple of acres. I shan't be idle in my retirement, and my wife can't wait for the day."

"Well, according to my mother, gardening is the best therapy in the world. Are you an experienced hand at it?"

"I've always dabbled. Never had much time. Always wanted to grow alpines. And my wife wants home grown vegetables. So I shall be busy enough."

"Have you told Conrad?"

"Not yet. He won't grieve. He likes John, who handles him with kid gloves. Are you going to have it out with him?"

"Yes."

"He'll cut the ground from under your feet. He'll be the hero, you the child he protected."

"I know. But I shall have my say. And give in my notice."

Brian Renfrow's eyebrows shot up.

"It means all that to you?"

"That he went behind my back to damage my friends for his own ends, yes."

He nodded, and began to stow papers in his brief-case.

"Unless you wanted Conrad to feed on you into his dotage, I think you're wise. You have a life of your own to live. A talent of your own to use. Good luck. I'm afraid it will not be a happy parting. When Conrad's hurt, he can be spiteful."

"I shall be sorry. I don't forget his kindness and generosity over the years."

"The balance of benefits was in his favour. Well, the old order changeth. You and I both off the scene. Look me up in Dorset if you're down that way. I'll send you my new address. I'll be seeing you before you leave, though, I expect."

"Yes, I shall give a month's notice and stay longer to train a successor if necessary."

After he had gone, Josephine made herself a pot of tea and nerved herself to tackle Conrad as soon as he arrived back. His mood, unfortunately, was not propitious, for the inspector of taxes had annoyed him exceedingly, and she waited for his acid comments to die down. It would perhaps have been wiser to wait until the next morning, but she wanted it over. She had rehearsed her opening speech over her cup of tea, and she began quietly.

"Mr. Ravensburg, I've something I have to discuss with you if you can spare the time now."

"Of course, my dear Josephine. Anything to take the taste of that obdurate, self-righteous, pompous little man away."

"It's not very pleasant, I'm afraid. It's to do with Mike Wexford. A week or two ago, I met the woman who had been Dr. Wexford's housekeeper, and she made some rather disquieting disclosures."

"Has that fellow turned up again to bother you, then?"

"No," said Josephine, and went on to tell him what she had learned from Mrs. Waycross and Dr. Wexford.

His reaction had been as she and Brian Renfrow had anticipated. In fact, she thought wearily, I could have spoken the lines for him. After painting himself as Sir Lancelot and finding her unimpressed, he went on, frowning a little,

"My dear girl, if I was mistaken, I'm sorry, but I think you must have forgotten just how distressed and nervy you were at that time."

"No, I haven't forgotten. You had no right to spread slanderous stories about Mike. He and his father had been friends of my family for years. It was my concern, not yours. And you cleverly concealed from me everything you did, even to muzzling the talk by the time we got back so that I never knew anything about it, only that Mike and his father had both left the district."

"Well, if that's all you can say about my efforts to save you trouble, I can only wonder at your attitude. It's not like you to be so irrational. Not like you at all. Why rake up this old business now? Why blame me for idle gossip?"

"Started by Mrs. Midhurst on your instructions."

"This has been a very trying day, Josephine. I really can't stay and listen to any more foolish complaints from you about a little incident that happened so long ago that I can't remember the details. If I was too zealous on your behalf, then I apologise. Now let's drop it. If you've any letters for me to sign, I'll have them now, and I can do with a cup of tea after dealing with that insufferable bureaucrat."

"I'll make a pot of tea straight away. Meanwhile, will you please accept my notice?" she said calmly, thinking that if that old deception was a matter of no importance to him, this might convince him that she was in earnest. But it didn't.

"Come, come, my dear. Don't pretend to be so put out as that." He was actually smiling. "We'll talk about it again tomorrow if you're not satisfied. But why it should bother you now, after all this time, I really don't know, unless you've taken up with that chap again," he added more sharply.

"You don't imagine that Mike Wexford will ever have anything to do with me again, after what happened, do you?"

"Well, you should be grateful to me for that," he said waspishly.

"I'll work out my month's notice, of course, and if you want me to stay on longer to train my successor, I'll do so."

"You don't really mean that?"

"I do."

"You're crazy. I can't believe this is my Josephine. Just because of a little misunderstanding years ago, when you were an inexperienced child?"

"No. Just because of deception, slander, and a lack of integrity. I've always admired you so much. At first I couldn't believe it of you. But I can't put the rose-coloured spectacles back. I must go."

For the first time since she had joined him, she saw the charming façade crack.

"After all I've done for you! Trained you, shown you the world, brought you out socially, paid you well. You can't do this to me, Josephine."

Because it was panic she saw looking out of his eyes, she spoke gently.

"I'm sorry, but I must. I've worked for you for four years to the best of my ability. But I didn't sign on for life, to have my personal affairs arranged for me as well as my business life. I can't work for you any longer. You may think I'm making a mountain out of a molehill. I can't see it like that. To me, it's something fundamental. A question of integrity."

She sat still while the tirade that followed rolled over her head. A master of words, he could use them as a lash most effectively, and she was white and trembling, but unshaken in her resolve, when he slammed out of the room. She tidied her desk, telephoned Mrs. Midhurst to bring Conrad a tray of tea, and walked out, leaving three letters for him to sign on his desk. He was on the telephone, and ignored her as she said good-night.

On the uphill path home, she sat down on the seat near the top, her legs feeling suddenly weak. This seat seemed significant. It was where she had broken with Mike, where she had sat in the spring in a mood of happy complacency, and where she now tried to recover after that ugly scene with her employer, and face the even more difficult prospect of trying to get the truth through to Mike. Between them, she was beginning to feel rather battered. But, she told herself briskly, she had lived in her cosy little world long enough. Time she had her eyes opened and grew up. But for all that, she quailed a little at the recollection of the anger in Mike's dark blue eyes, and wondered how she was going to get a hearing.

\*    \*    \*

92

Her telephone call to Mike was ineffective, as she had expected. There was nothing he wished to discuss with her ever again, he said, and rang off. The letter she wrote asking for just one meeting, after which she would trouble him no further, remained unanswered. She thought of appealing to Hester for aid, but rejected this idea, not wanting to involve her in any trouble with Mike, and not wishing to make known the past to her, since the last thing Mike would welcome would be any further publicising of his affairs among his new circle of friends. Finally, she appealed to the only other person who might be able to help her, Dr. Wexford. He answered her letter by return.

Dear Jo,

Mike is coming down for the last weekend in the month, arriving on Friday evening, departing Monday morning. As you are obviously so desperately anxious to see him, and I'm not sure that this is wise, you could call on one of those days, and I will arrange matters so that you find him alone. Let me know.

I hope things may work out satisfactorily, but am pretty sure that I shall be in the doghouse for my part! However, if you are prepared to face his wrath, I can, since he has an endearing way of letting me down lightly. I don't want you to get hurt, my dear, so think carefully about it. Sadly, we cannot unmake the past.

My kind regards to your mother.

Yours sincerely,
Robert Wexford.

Since she would not ask Conrad for time off, and indeed in his present icy, formal mood he would certainly have refused it, she took the Friday night train to Cornwall. She arrived at the Lenstow hotel in time for breakfast, and hired a taxi to drive her to Mawnsey, feeling tired and tense after a restless night in the sleeper when she had gone over and over in her mind the best way to tackle Mike. When the taxi dropped her outside Tamarisk Cottage, her courage almost failed her, drained as she was by the past two weeks with Conrad, on top of the private worries, for he had piled work ruthlessly on to her in an endeavour to get as much cleared as possible before she left. A part-time typist was due to start on Monday, and she would have to be guided as far as possible during the remaining two weeks. Conrad had left her to arrange this as a temporary measure as he had not decided what his future plans would be, and had no intention of discussing them with Josephine anyway, since she now appeared to be a criminal in his eyes. If she had retained any shreds of the rosy veils through which she had seen him in the past, these had now gone to the wind, and his barbed tongue had left wounds.

She had arranged to arrive at ten o'clock, and was only a few minutes late as she knocked at the door, feeling as though her legs were made of sawdust. Mike himself opened it. In navy blue roll-top sweater, navy trousers and canvas shoes, he had changed from lawyer to Cornishman. She could read nothing from his expression. It was as stony as Brighton beach.

"Come in," he said briefly, and led her to the sitting-room, indicating a chair. He posted himself on the hearth-rug, back to the fireplace, and thrust his hands in his pockets.

"This was sprung on me by my father just after breakfast. I've nothing to say to you and can't imagine why you've come, but I stayed in because he asked me to. He and my aunt have gone to the village. I'll give you fifteen minutes, Josephine, to say what you want to say, and then go."

It was only the recollection of the old Mike she had glimpsed at the cricket match that kept her from walking out on this arrogant, unyielding stranger. She drew a deep breath and said quietly,

"I want to tell you what has happened in the past few weeks to open my eyes about matters that concern you. You may or may not believe it, but I must tell you in the hope that you will. I'll be as brief as I can."

She kept to the facts, and when she looked up at him at the end of her recital, she could still read nothing from his expression. His dark blue eyes met hers in a probing scrutiny.

"Do you believe me?" she asked desperately.

"Why have you gone to all this trouble to tell me now?"

"To remove some of the bitterness from the past. Why else? And you haven't answered my question."

"Yes," he said quietly. "Yes, I believe you, though it's hard to credit Ravensburg's behaviour unless you gave him some grounds for it."

"It should have been harder to believe that of me."

"It was. Very, very hard."

"Oh, Mike, I'm sorry," she said, her eyes filling with tears.

He went to the window and stood gazing out. He's still not entirely convinced, she thought, blinking back her tears.

"Well, the grass has grown over that grave. Let's forget it now, shall we? Our paths have taken us in different directions."

"But we can meet now without strain and hostility?"

"All civilised, like polite divorcees? I guess so. There's

no putting the clock back, though, Jo. We're different,
people now."

"I know. But we can wipe out the past without
bitterness, I hope."

"Sure. You're still engrossed in your job?"

She stared at him, amazed. Did he think she was so
much a tool in Conrad's hands? That it meant nothing to
her, what he had done?

"Do you think I could go on working for him, knowing
what he did?"

He turned from the window then, eyes alert.

"You've left him?"

"I've two more weeks of my notice to work out."

"And then?"

"I've no definite plans. Some free-lance work to tide me
over, perhaps. I've had no thought for the future. I had to
get this mess sorted out first."

"I'm glad. And a little surprised. I thought he had you
nicely sewn up for life. A seductive prospect, after all."

"It's been an interesting job."

"And has put a fine polish on you."

"Glossy was the term," she said coolly.

"Back to form. So it was. But native honesty has
survived, I think. You look all in. I guess you could do
with a cup of coffee."

"Yes, please. I'm a bit short on sleep."

He looked at her white cheeks, the dark shadows under
her eyes, and said,

"Needless to say, that man turned nasty when challeng-
ed."

"Yes."

"He's well equipped for it. I'll get some coffee."

While he was absent, she leaned her head against the

96

back of the chair, feeling utterly spent, only gradually letting relief seep into her like warmth into frozen limbs.

Over coffee, they chatted about his job and his father's retirement, both feeling their way warily. Then she stood up to go. He did not try to detain her.

"Thank you for putting the record straight, Jo. For me, the broken engagement was a bad business anyway, but to know that it was a clean break makes the picture less ugly, and easier to forget. Something that happened a long time ago."

"The summer paths we used to know."

"Come again."

"Just a line from a poem that came into my head."

"When do you go back?"

"Tomorrow morning. The early train. I used a taxi to get here and plan to walk back round the cliffs. Where do I pick up the path?"

He told her and she went on her way, feeling strangely blank, so that she walked down to the little harbour and found the path behind the inn scarcely taking in her surroundings. The track went uphill and down following the contours of the cliff, through golden brown bracken on to springy turf broken by huge mounds of thrift with pale papery flower heads and patches of purple thyme. Far below, the waves broke on little sandy bays caught between the rearing cliffs in pristine peace and beauty.

Half way back, she sat down to rest against a hummock of thrift and watched the waves below, feeling the spell of the Cornish coast as an invitation to forget the small troubles of insignificant humans and become absorbed in the natural world. That was what her mother had done after her father had died. Contracted out. But her mother's natural world was very tiny, the size of a garden.

She plucked at a piece of grass, not able to escape so easily, aware of an odd sense of loss. She had done what she had to do, Mike had accepted her explanation, but she was still the girl who had turned him down long ago and gone her own way, as he had done. Ways that had taken them far apart. But she was beginning to realise now that deep in her heart was the wish to go back to meet him, to rediscover the man, Mike Wexford. It was only Mike's back, though, that she could see in the distance.

She watched a small launch come round the headland, bucketing through the waves. Something in the stance of the man at the wheel told her that it was Mike. There was another man in the rear doing something with a rope. Spray leapt up round the bows of the launch as it went out to round the next headland, and then disappeared. It seemed symbolic.

I was too young, Mike. Far too young for you then. You should have been more patient. She sat there unaware of the passage of time until the freshening breeze awoke her to the fact that she was cold, and she walked on briskly towards Lenstow, but she did not see the launch again.

# 9

# New Moves

Josephine's last two weeks at Valery Mount were not made more pleasant by the brash confidence of the twenty-year-old part-time typist who knew it all, and had no disposition to learn the finer points of the job in prospect. She had already sampled many different kinds of work in her short career since leaving a commercial training college, and was, Josephine suspected, a confirmed flitter from job to job. However, Conrad had indicated that he only needed a stop-gap until he had made up his mind about future plans, and Miss Hillsdale, competent enough on a typewriter, would doubtless suffice.

Conrad's mood was not improved by the folding of his play after only one month, but he was cheered a few days later by the news that Renfrow had brought the subsidiary rights deal to a successful conclusion. This good news, however, did not soften his attitude to Josephine, who was given a very stiff and brief goodbye. Speaking on the telephone to Brian Renfrow on her last afternoon, she learned that Conrad was now talking of moving to Jersey, to avoid the penal taxation which he so much resented.

"The good news today has reinforced the idea," said Renfrow. "Has he discussed it with you?"

"No. I've been in the doghouse for the past month."

"You're well out of it, my dear. He owes you a lot, though. Petty of him to behave like this."

And so she left Valery Mount for the last time and

called at the flat to leave a book on cricket for Barry, who opened his eyes and flushed with pleasure at this unexpected gift.

"I'm sorry you're leaving, Miss Riverton. That young woman who's taking your place won't last long, I'm thinking. A bold one, that. I doubt whether this post will give her what she wants. Even Bill Mendon feels threatened," added Mrs. Midhurst with a wry humour which surprised Josephine. Could Hilda Midhurst be thawing just a little?

Barry walked to the front gate with her.

"I wish you weren't going," he observed, scowling as he kicked a stone along the drive.

"But I live in Elmfield. I'll be seeing you around. We'll have another day at a cricket match next summer, shall we?"

He nodded, giving her his sudden sweet smile, and swung on the gate, watching her walk down the lane. She wondered what would happen to Mrs. Midhurst and Barry if Conrad moved to Jersey. Once people were of no more use to him, it seemed, Conrad's generosity and consideration faded.

\* \* \*

The following week, Josephine spent an evening with Hester and discussed the future with her.

"I'd like to have a stab at free-lancing to see if I can earn a living at it. I've some reserves to keep me going for a time. I earned good money with Conrad Ravensburg and reckon I can give myself a trial run of six months."

"Good idea. I'm all for being one's own boss. Free-lancing's not easy these days, though. Any contacts?" asked Hester, presiding over the coffee pot.

"The editor of the local paper I used to work for. He edits a country magazine now and would be glad to see any articles I care to submit. He taught me my job and knows my work, and was encouraging when I spoke to him yesterday."

"Good. Now let me see. Who do I know who might be useful? There's Nick Barbury. He has a lot of contacts. Used to edit an arts magazine himself before he took off as a biographer. He might have some helpful suggestions. I'll phone him and find out."

"Thanks, Hester. It's good of you to bother."

"No bother. You need some new interests, I fancy. You look a bit peaky. Anything wrong?"

"The sour taste of disillusion. Conrad was my hero when I first worked for him. Even after four years of close companionship with him, I retained a good deal of that early admiration. The hero's mould cracked badly at the end, though, and it came as rather a shock."

Hester's dark eyes surveyed Josephine thoughtfully. Then she said,

"Well, I've always found work the best antidote to depression. Get cracking on those articles. Doesn't matter what articles, whether you can sell them or not, get down to it. Writing's a marvellous therapy. Lose yourself in it."

"I'll try."

"You're too much of an idealist, you know. Just bear in mind that in ninety-nine cases out of a hundred, men are poor material for hero-worshippers."

Josephine smiled. Hester's resistance to male charms was formidable, although she numbered a good many men among her friends.

"How do you manage it, Hester? To be friendly and yet not get emotionally involved?"

"I have work that absorbs and satisfies me. The trouble with most women is that they don't have that. Things are improving in that direction, but too much of women's work is still boring, doesn't stretch them or fulfil their potentialities in any way, and so they pin their thoughts on men. Too much emotional concentration. Bad for both of them."

"I'll see if I can develop your admirable detachment. It sounds simple, but I'm sure it isn't."

"Well, perhaps it's simpler to listen to the voice of reason when you're in your forties than in your twenties. I fear you're handicapped with too tender a heart. You need tougher fibres in place of those sensitive threads of yours."

"Like coconut matting, you mean?"

"Exactly," said Hester, glad to see the laughter back in Josephine's eyes.

"How snug you are here, Hester," observed Josephine sinking back in her armchair with a second cup of coffee.

"M'm. About to leave the snuggery for rugged Cornwall next week, though. I've got a bit bogged down with my current book. It's set in Cornwall, and I need to refresh my mind about the background, get the feel of it."

"Whereabouts in Cornwall?"

"North coast. Half way between Lenstow and Mawnsey. A farmhouse set back from the cliffs, with room for a few guests in the summer. Mike introduced me to it when I was down that way last June. He was spending the weekend with his father, and we had a day's walking along the cliffs, ending in a marvellous cream tea at this farmhouse. They can let me have a bedroom and a room for working in, and I plan to spend a month there, getting this book moving."

"You shouldn't be troubled with holiday crowds at this time of the year."

"It's always pretty quiet on that stretch, anyway."

Driving home, Josephine found herself envying Hester's ordered life, her certainty about what she wanted, her success in achieving it. She and Mike seemed to have established a good friendship. She was ten years older than he, and perhaps he found this a safer proposition than loving a young girl who had a change of heart and sent him packing after years of friendship. But she hadn't meant it to be like that. He had made no effort to get in touch with her again after their meeting at his father's home. The past was finished with, he seemed to say. And perhaps he still felt that she had been disloyal, even if not as culpable as Conrad's actions had seemed to indicate. It would not be unreasonable of him to think that she must in some way have made Conrad think him a violent threat, even if only by implication.

She sighed, wishing that she could dismiss Mike from her thoughts, could lose this sad sense of loss that haunted her.

A few days later, Nick Barbury telephoned her and asked her to have lunch with him in London. They could have a chat, and he might be able to advise her on suitable markets for her work. She thanked him and they made an appointment to meet at the National Gallery.

He was waiting for her, fair, handsome, elegant, in a pale grey suit with a dashing purple and grey tie. It was a mild day of pale sunshine, and she was wearing a trim navy coat with a jade green collar over a matching green dress, wishing to please her companion's well known sartorial fastidiousness, and the approval which she read in his eyes as he greeted her did her confidence, which had been faltering lately, a power of good.

He took her to an Italian restaurant where the food was delectable, and the wine as smooth as silk although she was not sufficient of a connoisseur to judge its finer points. The restaurant had an intimate atmosphere, with tables in alcoves, and much red carpet and brass about. She gave Nick a detailed account of past experience, and discussed her ideas about the type of articles she felt able to supply.

"It's a difficult market to break into," he observed. "Most magazines have their regular contributors and don't stray outside. I can give you one or two introductions that might be useful, though."

They went on to talk about books and authors, and in no time at all, an hour and a half had sped by. When, outside the restaurant, Josephine thanked him, she gave him her warmest smile.

"You don't know how much you've cheered me up. I've been a bit becalmed in the doldrums lately. This meeting has really put some wind back in my sails."

"My pleasure. I'll be interested to know how you get on. Are you sure I can't call a taxi to take you to Victoria?"

"Quite sure, thank you. I've some shopping to do. Books I want to buy."

"No more enjoyable way of spending an afternoon than browsing in bookshops. I've an appointment to keep, or I'd join you. Good luck, Josephine. Has anybody ever told you that you have the most delightful smile? I'm sure they have. *Adios*."

He surprised her then by taking her by the shoulders and kissing her cheek before lifting his hand in a final salute and going on his way. There was no doubt, she thought as she walked off in the direction of her favourite bookshop in Piccadilly, that Nicholas Barbury was a great charmer, and a first-rate tonic for a downcast ego.

She picked up her car at Dilford Station and drove home in the dusk of the evening, which did not prevent her from seeing a large For Sale notice at the entrance to Valery Mount. So Conrad was moving. He had not wasted much time. And again she wondered about the fate of Mrs. Midhurst and Barry. This was made clear to her on the following Sunday morning when she met Bill Mendon and Barry walking along the edge of a strip of woodland at the foot of the downs. Barry was picking up conkers, and when he saw her, he ran excitedly to her, his pockets bulging.

"I've got a dad," he said, his usual stolid, cautious manner quite overlaid.

"Have you?" said Josephine, startled.

"Yes. Mr. Mendon."

"You're a bit premature, son," said Bill Mendon, his eyes twinkling. "You run off and finish collecting your conkers while Miss Riverton and I have a chat."

Barry lumbered off, scuffling up leaves with gusto as he went. Bill Mendon, clad in an old tweed jacket over corduroy trousers, and a battered felt hat with a jay's feather tucked into its band, turned his weather-beaten face to Josephine and grinned at her amazed expression.

"What did he mean?" she asked.

"Why, that I'm marrying his mum a month come Saturday. That surprises you, I guess," he said, chuckling.

"More than somewhat. I can quite see why Barry's so happy, though. Tell me more."

"Well, you know Mr. Ravensburg's moving to Jersey?"

"I had heard it suggested."

"Told Mrs. Midhurst she must look out for a new post. She was right upset. It's not easy, with a boy Barry's age, and no home of your own. Well, since me mother died last January, it's been a bit bleak in the cottage. And me and Hilda Midhurst have got to understand each other pretty well over the years. The kid needs a dad. So I says to myself, why don't we get together?"

"I hope you'll be very happy, Bill. It's splendid news for Barry. You've done so much for him."

"Aye. He's not had much of a deal from life, I guess. Nor won't have, the world being what it is. I'm fond of the kid. I know what you're thinking, though," he added, chuckling again. "That Hilda's not exactly a cosy woman. But she's a good sort, in her way. A bit of a puritan, but I guess she'll mellow a bit when she's got a place of her own. She's a good cook and she'll keep the cottage nice. I like a well-kept home. Me mother always kept it nice. I'd be glad to see it properly looked after. Not much of a hand at domestic crafts myself. I guess Hilda will make a good job of it, and keep me in me place," he concluded with a wink which suggested that nobody would succeed in downing this little Yorkshireman.

"Well, I'm very pleased, Bill. Although I couldn't be more surprised, I think you have a recipe for a satisfactory solution to the problems of all concerned. Of course, I don't really know Mrs. Midhurst. She's not easy to know."

"Keeps herself to herself. Had a tough time when she was a young woman. We don't enquire into that too closely. But it's amazing what a bit of security will do. And a bit of independence. A proud woman. Hasn't been easy for her to have no base of her own, and saddled with the boy, too. I don't expect Paradise, you know. Seen too much of the world to expect that. But I reckon it'll work out quite well."

"I reckon it will," said Josephine. "And what about your job now that Mr. Ravensburg is leaving? Will you stay on if the new owners want you?"

"No. Aim to start a little market garden business with a pal of mine. I inherited a bit from me mum. The old girl bought that rough land at the back of the cottage some years ago. Never done anything with it, except let it out for pony grazing. She was a shrewd one, the old lady. Got it dirt cheap. Five acres. I reckon I can make it pay, and perhaps the kid will take to the work. Give him some sort of a future, a chance to earn a living. He's not bright at school, you know. Prospects for anything but a labourer's job pretty dim. He likes being out of doors. I can train him, I guess."

"You're very fond of him, aren't you?"

"Well, I've been a bit of a misfit myself, so I know what it's like."

"I think his luck's turned now."

"You've been kind to him, Miss Riverton. That gets good marks in my book. Easy to give treats to kids with winning ways and pretty faces. Barry's sort usually get left out. To hear the village talk, you'd think I was taking on a delinquent. And a shrew. They're so sorry for me, I've been stood more pints of bitter at the pub than a local hero," he concluded, chuckling again.

"I think you've got everything well in hand, Bill," said Josephine, laughing.

"I'm not bothered. Barry," he called, "stop pelting that squirrel. He's doing you no harm. Not that he'll hit him in a month of Sundays," added Bill Mendon as the squirrel leapt from bough to bough above Barry's head.

"With a business of your own, what about those cricket matches?"

107

"We'll call Hilda in to take over while we're away." he said, winking.

Josephine went on her way, smiling, glad to think that Barry's future looked so much brighter. It was a calm, clear November day, the air crisp, and she had the path to herself as she climbed up to the crest of the downs. It was a steep pull, and she paused at the top and leaned against a stile. It was very quiet up there. Now and again she heard a snatch of song from a lark, the sound of sheep in the distance. The smooth, bare contours of the downs, with their folds and rounded crests, lay all around her, while far ahead she could see a small glittering strip, like a mirror, reminding her that wherever you walked on these downs, the sea was not far away. Mike had leaned on this same stile one hot July day studying the map, and she had taken his photograph. They had walked on to that spinney for some shade in which to eat their lunch. And afterwards, he had asked her to marry him and she had said yes. No passionate declaration of love. No stumbling, emotional phrases. Matter-of-fact, sure-footed. And he had been given a simple, unhesitating answer. That was how it had been between them. And on that day, the larks had been singing gloriously and unceasingly high in the sky above.

The trouble with the downs, peaceful and lovely as they were, was that they were so full of memories. She had shared them with Mike for so long. And, as always when looking back, it was the sunny days she remembered.

She climbed the stile and walked on, wondering why she should feel so disappointed that Mike had made no attempt to get in touch with her. Putting herself in his place, why should he want to be reminded of a painful rejection, of places where his name had been bandied

108

about by all and sundry, his most intimate feelings the subject of public discussion? She could not remedy that. It had happened. And in his place, she would want no reminders. Love died under that kind of hammering. And she realised for the first time as she walked on alone that love put a heavy responsibility on one's shoulders, for the hurt you inflicted on someone who loved you struck so deeply, as the doctor had said. If Mike had not loved her so dearly, the episode would have been unpleasant, damaging to pride, but would have been written off in time as hard experience. But loving her as he did, the wound had been mortal. That was something she had to accept.

# 10
# *Accident in Cornwall*

The letter from Hester arrived on a grey, drizzling morning half way through November.

Dear Jo,

I am typing this S.O.S. painfully with one finger as I had a fall down a cliff yesterday and have damaged both hands and arms and one leg! My brain is still intact, though, and wanting to get on with my book and stop feeling the pain of these wretched limbs. As you are a free woman just now, would you be willing to come down here and act as my secretary? Take the place of my arms and leg?

They can put you up here. It is very comfortable. All expenses mine, of course, plus a salary we can discuss if you are willing.

If not convenient, shall quite understand. I spoke to Mike on the telephone yesterday evening. He will be ringing you to fill you in on the details and save me trying to tap out more. I didn't telephone you because I never think it's fair to spring this sort of proposition on people without giving them time to think. Perhaps you'd ring me. Don't hesitate to turn it down if you are otherwise occupied.

Flaming mad with myself! Hope all is well with you, and journalistic prospects good.

                                                                    Yours,
                                                                    Hester

Mike telephoned her that same evening. He was very business-like.

"This proposition of Hester's. Are you willing?"

"Of course. Reading between the lines of her letter, I'd say she's in a fix."

"Yes. I was going down to see my father this coming weekend, anyway. Hester suggested that if you can help her out, it would be best for you to come down with me, and use her car down there, and drive her back in due course if she can't drive herself. Are you in agreement?"

She wished he wouldn't talk to her like a lawyer to a client.

"It seems a sensible arrangement."

"Right. Can you be ready at six o'clock on Saturday morning? That should get us down there about mid-afternoon."

"I'll be ready. It will save time if I bring a packed lunch, won't it?"

"Yes, do that. We'll have breakfast on the road. I'll telephone the farmhouse and say you'll be coming. It's a well-run place. You'll be comfortable there."

"Mike, do you think Hester's badly hurt? She's the sort to make light of it."

"When Hester's in the throes of a book, her body is of no importance. As long as she's not in agony, she'll ignore it. I've asked my father to look in. Hester has met him and they get on very well, so she'll probably let him examine her. I bet she hasn't seen a doctor. Doesn't believe in 'em. She's a nature-cure believer, and could well be sitting on a fracture without doing a thing about it."

"Well, your father has a way with him, too. A contest between Hester and him will be quite something. I'm glad he's at hand. I can't help feeling a bit worried."

"At six on Saturday, then."

\* \* \*

It was dark and cold on that Saturday morning when Josephine walked down the path and slid into the car beside Mike, who had kept the engine running. She had been waiting for him and emerged as soon as the car drew up, dead on time. He put her case on the back seat, with the shopping basket containing their lunch. She wondered if he was thinking back across the years to the many times when she had sat beside him in the old Morris. A more powerful car now, an impersonal stranger driving, herself caught in a strange feeling of unreality. She couldn't behave like an acquaintance, nor could she rescue the old familiarity to ease the situation. She had learned during the years with Conrad to handle most situations with tact and poise, but this one found her constrained and edgy. The intimacy between them had been so complete, the subsequent gulf so deep and bitter, that now she could only grope, feeling tension building up inside her as they left Elmfield behind them. Perhaps it was easier for Mike, who was occupied with the driving. She clasped her gloved hands tightly, reminding herself that they were going to spend some nine hours shut up together in this car, and she'd better get a grip of herself and play it calmly.

"Nice car," she said, appreciating the silkiness of the engine, the power which made driving so much easier.

"M'm. Made the change when I realised I'd have a lot of long distance motoring to do with my father living in Cornwall."

"Do you go down often?"

"Every month or so. The old man was lonely at first, a bit cut off. He's adjusted to it happily now, but I like to get down there whenever I can. Cornwall's always had a hold on me."

And he had no need to tell her that, she thought. How odd it was, talking as though they were mere acquaintances. Perhaps that was the only tolerable way for him now.

"A long journey to do at one stretch."

"I like driving. I travel by night in the summer when holiday-makers make the day trip tedious. It's going to be a long day. Why don't you have a kip in the back until it's light?"

"I'll have a cat-nap where I am. It's very comfortable," she said.

"You can adjust the rake of the seat with that lever just beside you."

"It's fine as it is." she said, leaning back and closing her eyes, as far from a nap as a tiger pacing up and down in a cage. However, if it would spare him the duty of polite discourse, she was willing to simulate sleep.

Dawn broke as they were running across a stretch of heathland, the rising sun flooding the landscape with light and warmth for a brief period until it vanished behind a bank of cloud, and a uniform greyness took over. They stopped at a hotel in Winchester for breakfast. It was obviously Mike's usual port of call, for the porter knew him, and gave him a cheerful welcome. Josephine, finding herself hungry, made a determined effort to relax over the scrambled eggs and coffee. The trouble was, she thought, they had known each other too well for superficial exchanges, but had lost their way with each other. Food seemed to have a mellowing effect on Mike, too, for he began to ask her about her prospects as a journalist, and to look at her as though he at least knew her.

"Too soon to say," she replied in answer to his enquiry, "but I've a firm commission for a column each month for my old editor, who now runs a country magazine, and hopeful noises coming from an editor Nick Barbury introduced. I don't suppose I shall be able to make any sort of permanent living out of it, but it will tide me over for a time. I don't know how long Hester will want me. Hope your father didn't find too much damage."

"She's not young or agile enough to go scrambling on those cliffs."

"It's not like her. She's not an outdoor type at all."

"She was checking up on the plausibility of some incident in her book. Likes to re-enact it to get the details right. Make it more graphic, she says. And to do that, Hester would climb Everest if necessary," he concluded drily.

"She's a dear," said Josephine, smiling. "And far too independent to take any cautionary advice."

"You're telling me. Intelligent as a monkey, and as difficult to pin down. She makes every one of my father's hairs stand on end with her views on health practices, and he is not a narrow-minded man, as you know."

It's getting easier, thought Josephine, as she passed him a second cup of coffee. We're talking as though we've met before. She wondered if it would be too dangerous to tell him that he looked tired. Too personal. But he did. She noticed with a pang the deep lines running from nostril to mouth, the prominence of the cheek-bones. A powerful face, she thought, with those heavy black brows, firm mouth, square chin. Fine dark blue eyes his best feature.

And a lean, strong build, emphasised that morning by a heavy grey tweed jacket over a blue roll-top sweater. Thick black hair, difficult to control. She flushed as he looked up suddenly and caught her scrutiny.

"How are affairs at Romsey and Wexford?" she asked hastily.

"Busy."

"Pleasantly, or under pressure? I thought," she added carefully, "that you looked a bit tired."

"A difficult case is causing us some headaches just now. Been working late at it."

"This weekend isn't exactly timely, then."

"Oh, a break may clear my head," he said with a little smile. "Ready?"

They stopped for lunch on a narrow, winding road across Dartmoor. The sun had struggled through again, shining warmly through the windscreen. Beside them, a low stone wall topped by bare beech trees bordered the road, while ahead of them and to the other side stretched the combes and hills of the moor, a harmony of muted colours, the gold brown of bracken, the darker brown of dead heather, and here and there a vivid patch of green moss and grass.

With the centre arm of the car-seats pushed up, the small basket between them, they worked their way through ham sandwiches, sausage rolls, tomatoes, and an apple and banana apiece. A flask of coffee completed their meal.

"Isn't it astonishing how hungry one gets just sitting in a car making no physical effort whatever?" observed Josephine, manipulating the flask of coffee.

"All goes to confirm Hester's denigration of the value of physical exercise. Is that a sausage roll you missed?"

She retrieved it from a corner of the basket, and handed it to him.

"Halves?" he asked.

"No. You have it."

"Your mother's make?"

"No, mine. Now that I work for myself, I have more time for such pursuits."

"Your mother has passed on her light touch with pastry. I still remember the incredible, melting mince pies she used to make."

"Cooking and gardening are her specialities. She's equally good at both."

"Think I'll go for a stroll and stretch my legs. You might like to catch up on the news," he added, passing her the copy of *The Times* which he had bought in Winchester.

We mustn't get too friendly, she thought wryly, chilled by the hand-off just as the atmosphere seemed to be getting warmer.

He walked off down a heathery slope towards the stream at the bottom. When he was out of sight, she slid out of the car and walked along the deserted road in the opposite direction. On her way back, she stopped and leaned on a gate while she watched a hawk hovering high above her. It swooped suddenly, with a swiftness she could scarcely follow, then soared again with some luckless prey, too far off for her to distinguish what it was. Probably an unwary field-mouse. The sun had disappeared behind grey clouds again and the moor looked bleak and desolate. Saddened by the constrained atmosphere between herself and Mike, wishing she could find the way back to him, she returned to the car to find him already in the driving seat.

"By the way," he said, "does Hester know our previous history?"

"No, of course not. I haven't discussed it with her or any of our new circle of friends. Why should I?"

"I just wondered. I know you and she are good friends now. Thought you might indulge in heart-to-hearts."

"She would hardly have suggested this project if she'd known about the past. She's not that tactless."

He nodded, but said nothing, and put the car into gear. She felt annoyed that he should think her a prattler about such painful, intimate history, and said a little tartly,

"I presume you've been similarly reticent."

"There was more than enough talk about it at the time. As far as I'm concerned, the subject was done to death then and buried. I'd no more think of talking about it than I'd sit in a graveyard digging up old bones."

The old bitterness was there, but Josephine was in no mood to pander to it, her nerves taut.

"That makes two of us then. I don't know why you had to raise it just now."

"My mistake. Say no more."

And for the rest of that journey their exchanges were few and frigidly polite.

The farmhouse, nestling in a hollow a few hundred yards back from the cliff edge, looked cheerful and welcoming on that gloomy, drizzly afternoon, for lights shone from several of the windows and the surrounding spinney of hawthorn and elderberry trees gave it a snug, protected air. The owner was a middle-aged man of square build and genial manner, who greeted Mike with pleased familiarity.

"My wife will show the young lady her room, and then

there's a good tea laid for you in Miss Northbridge's sitting-room."

They found Hester, swathed in bandages from shoulder to fingers of both arms and from thigh to ankle of one leg, lying on a sofa in front of a crackling fire. She looked white and drawn, but had a bright smile for them.

"Bless you both, am I glad to see you!" she said. "Sorry about my grotesque appearance. I feel like that advertisement for tyres—the Michelin man."

She refused to talk about her injuries until they had had tea.

"It's a hideously long journey to do in one day and you must be in dire need of refreshment. A cup of tea and one piece of toast is all I want, Jo, if you'll just put it on this little table, then you two can tuck in."

"Well, Jo brought along a pretty substantial picnic lunch, but I must say this looks tempting," said Mike, eyeing plates of scones and toast and bread and butter, a dish of jam and a pot of honey, a large fruit cake, a plate of jam tarts, and a bowl of cream.

Josephine seized on the large brown earthenware teapot and set to work, her eyes distressed as she saw the pain Hester tried to hide as she lifted her cup.

"Now, what's the real damage?" asked Mike when they had all but finished. "Did my father come over?"

"He did. He bandaged me up after I'd refused to go to a hospital. He doesn't think any bones are broken, just badly bruised, except for one finger, which is broken and which he's strapped up tightly. Wanted me to go to hospital for X-rays and anti-tetanus injection. We had a little tussle about it. He's a dear man. Not as hide-bound as most G.P.s. We remain friends," she concluded with a faint grin.

"How did it happen?" asked Mike.

"Well, I think a degree of amnesia has set in, because I'm a bit hazy. I was exploring a track down one of the cliff faces, seeing what kind of a surface the rock had, what would be involved in climbing it and so on, and all I remember is gingerly creeping nearly to the point where the track gave out. The rest is blank until I came to on a rocky ledge some distance below. Think I was a bit concussed, because some time had elapsed. I was a horrible bloody mess, and getting back was a nightmare. There wasn't anybody within earshot or within miles, I guess. Anyway, I got to the top in the end, and crawled to a lane, where a motorist eventually picked me up and brought me back here. Fortunately, Mrs. Rossland, the farmer's wife, was a trained nurse before she married so she did me up a treat," concluded Hester.

"I reckon you're lucky," observed Mike. "Those cliffs are not for amateurs. I could have told you anything you wanted to know about climbing them."

"But you were a long way away, and there's nothing like actual experience. I'm no end grateful to you for coming to my aid now, though. Began to think the book would die inside me before I could get it out."

Josephine shook her head at such a hopeless case, and realised that one way and another, she would have her hands full. Mike left them soon after, and Josephine went to her room to unpack. What an odd freak of destiny this was that had perforce thrown her back into Mike's company again, manifestly against his wish. Her hopes of their getting to know each other all over again now that the past had been explained seemed dim. For Mike, love had died, even liking had died. He wanted to be rid of her. Because of bitter memories? Because she had changed from the child he once knew and he had no wish to get to know the mature Josephine Riverton? She couldn't say. She only felt in her heart the dull ache of the loss.

# 11

# Christmas Revels

During the weeks that followed, Josephine found her duties as a nurse less rewarding than her duties as a secretary, for Hester was a difficult patient, but had the capacity to put pain and discomfort out of her mind when working, so that the book made good progress, while the physical damage was slow to mend.

"It's all in the mind," said Hester airily when Josephine tried to get her to go to the hospital for a check-up. "Nature will get me better in time. I don't want any potions, drugs or technological treatment which might delay the healing, if not do harm. We weren't born needing doctors, you know. The healing capacity was born within us."

"But if the pain keeps you from sleeping, nature's best card, rest, is missing."

"I find the wakeful hours of the night the most fruitful for unravelling my plot."

"You're a very stubborn character, Hester, and although I admire your grit, I deplore your neglect of yourself. You don't eat enough to keep a sparrow alive. You're not immune to the number one law of nature, that you need food to live," concluded Josephine with a firmness that brought a twinkle to Hester's eyes.

"Dear Jo. You're a wonderful help to me. If I didn't think that you ought to cultivate your own garden, because you've got a talent for writing yourself, I'd try to bribe you to be my permanent assistant."

"I know when I'm beaten. I think you'll want to change a good deal of yesterday's stint. It's a bit laboured."

"M'm. My brain seemed to be stuck in putty yesterday. Get days like that. I'll go over it after tea. Draw the curtains, Jo. I hate these short dark days of December."

With the curtains drawn, they shared the pot of tea which Mrs. Rossland had brought them. Hester, stretched out on the sofa, nibbled at a biscuit to placate Josephine, and ran her eye over the sheets of typescript.

"Yes, that's as heavy-footed as an elephant. I must give some thought to it. By the way," she added as she laid the sheets aside, "you know that pile of glossy magazines Mrs. Rossland brought up yesterday. There was an interesting photograph in one of them. Pass me the one on the top."

She leafed through the magazine and handed it to Josephine, open at a page of photographs taken at a theatrical function in London. An important occasion, with evening dress and white ties prevailing. Josephine's eyes skimmed over several famous faces in the acting profession until she came to one with the caption 'Penelope Rockdale with friend.' The friend, his hand on the elbow of the well known actress, was Mike.

"A dark horse, our Mike," said Hester. "I never knew he was friendly with my favourite actress. This was taken back in October."

"She's lovely, isn't she?" said Josephine, admiring the oval face with its classical features and smooth fair hair worn, ballerina style, on the top of her head.

"Yes. I'll never forget her as Candida. A truly great performance. Wonder how long Mike's known her. Has he ever mentioned her to you?"

"No."

"Oh well, our woman-hater has undoubted charm

himself. I've no doubt he has plenty of chances of enjoying his leisure with the despised sex when in the mood. They make an impressive pair," she added dispassionately.

"I saw her play Rosalind in *As You Like It* a year or two ago. She was captivating. I can't see how any man who knows her could help falling in love with her."

"Bless your romantic heart, she may be a shrew off the stage. I agree that the assets are considerable. I think our rugged Cornishman is in no danger of losing his head over any woman, whatever the assets, though. Enjoying them is another matter."

"You and Mike have a lot in common. Sceptics to the core," said Josephine, smiling to hide the wincing.

"Yes, we get on very well. We can be perfectly frank with each other with no offence taken. That's refreshing. Now let me see if I can kick some life into this," she added, picking up the typed pages.

Josephine left her to it and decided to go out for some air, for she was tied to the farmhouse more than she would have chosen by Hester's dependence on her.

The night was mild, and a half moon made it light enough to see her way along the footpath to the edge of the cliffs. Below her, a calm sea lapped the shore, but on this coast, she thought, the mighty force of the Atlantic seemed always present, even when quiescent. Her thoughts, as so often nowadays, turned to Mike. It was time, she decided, to try to reverse that state of affairs. He had made it obvious that he had finished with her when the engagement was broken and had no wish to renew even a mild friendship. Her explanation may have removed some of the unpleasant taste from the past, but it had come too late to warm any embers that might have remained of his love for her. She must accept that and not make pathetic efforts to fan them into life again. Whatever he had gone through at that time had changed him, changed his feelings about her, his attitude to women. She no longer knew him, and he had no wish that she should. It was no use shirking that knowledge.

Alone there on the cliffs that night, she accepted the reality of the situation, banishing her hopes of reconciliation, of finding a way back to those old summer paths, as romantic dreams. She would be better advised to turn her attention to her work as a journalist in whatever time was left over to her after looking after Hester, and there and then she decided to pay a last tribute to those old paths with a nostalgic article on the Sussex Downs in summer recollected in the darkness of December days. And after that, there must be no more looking back, no more fretting for what could not be.

\*     \*     \*

Hester's progress was slow, as the broken finger and the wrenched knee kept her more or less immobilised, although the bruised bones were easing and she felt better in herself. It was obvious that she would have to spend Christmas in Cornwall, but she reckoned on being able to get home early in January.

"I've no right to keep you here over Christmas, Jo," she said, "but if you could stay, I'd be very glad. Dr. Wexford looked in while you were out this morning, and suggested that we might care to spend Christmas Day with them. Mike will be coming down, and he'll transport me. But if you've other commitments, you must say. I shall be able to manage."

"I don't know about leaving my mother alone at

124

Christmas," said Josephine doubtfully. "For myself, I'd happily stay here. I'll telephone her and have a chat."

On the telephone that evening, her mother was emphatic.

"I never mind being on my own, darling, you know that. Stay with your friends. A much livelier prospect for you. I feel guilty about the dullness of a Christmas at home for you, but you know I'm no good at parties and can't face a lot of entertaining."

"I'm never dull at home with you. It's just that Hester still needs a helping hand. I shall be home for the New Year, anyway. But I don't like the thought of your being alone. Why not come down to Cornwall? I could fix you up here or at a hotel, and Dr. Wexford would be very pleased to see you again."

"That's a nice thought, dear, but no. As a matter of fact, my order for new roses hasn't turned up yet, but is due any time now, and I shall most likely spend Christmas planting them."

It was no use, thought Josephine. She would never winkle her mother out of her shell. She really had become a loner since she was widowed, and preferred it that way. Solitude and her mother were happy together, and she could understand that. Promising to telephone on Christmas morning, she rang off and settled for Christmas in Cornwall.

The weather over that Christmas was wet and windy, but they spent a happy day at Tamarisk Cottage with Dr. Wexford and his sister, Muriel, and the few friends they had invited. One of them, a dark, vivacious girl named Diana, the daughter of a neighbour, made a bee line for Mike, who seemed happy enough to play along with a faintly indulgent air that amused Josephine.

Hester, in much better form, had arranged a small party on Boxing-night as a thank you to the doctor, his sister, Mike and Josephine, for their help over the past weeks. She had booked a table at the Harbour Inn, where the Boxing-night dinner and dance was a well-attended annual event.

"I shall have to be an onlooker," observed Hester, testing her knee gingerly, "but that will suit me. You're a fetching sight for these old eyes, Jo," she added, her eyes approving the line of the willow-green dress, with its tight bodice, long narrow sleeves and flowing skirt. "A mediaeval touch. It suits you. Heavy medallions are what that neck calls for. Not that the silver chain isn't very suitable," she added hastily.

"Damning with faint praise," said Josephine, laughing. "I'll look for some medallions when I've time."

"There's quite a touch of red in your hair. Never noticed it before. I wonder some man hasn't snatched you up long before this. Ever been at risk?"

"Dozens of times," said Josephine solemnly as she handed Hester her walking stick.

"Should be a jolly evening. Good food, Mike says, and an old-fashioned style of dance that goes down well in these parts. I went there with him once for a drink. A real old smugglers' inn. The right atmosphere for Christmas, if you're a traditionalist."

And, indeed, the Harbour Inn might have been the prototype for hundreds of Christmas cards, with its small leaded-light windows, black oak beams, low ceiling, gleaming brass, holly and mistletoe abundant, old coaching prints on the panelled walls. There was a roaring log fire at one end of the room and a Christmas tree at the other. The tables were grouped round the perimeter of the

126

room, and the centre space was large enough to accommodate about ten couples for dancing. In the far corner a piano, and two chairs in front of music stands were occupied by a trio, chatting together and sorting out music as the meal progressed. At their table, close to the Christmas tree, Josephine had Dr. Wexford on her right and Hester on the left of her. Mike was the other side of Hester, but Josephine felt his presence with every fibre of her being. All very well to tell herself that there was nothing left between them, that she must learn to treat him as a casual acquaintance when they met, forget the past, but every time she came within yards of him, she was acutely conscious of his every movement.

She had kept up the light touch on the previous day, and he had been equally pleasant and detached, but it was difficult this evening, with the whole atmosphere conducive to warmth and relaxation.

"What is your mother doing this Christmas, my dear?" asked Dr. Wexford.

"Planting roses. When I phoned her yesterday morning, she said she was having a lovely Christmas, alone in the garden. It was mild and drizzly, she said. Just right for planting. She's incorrigible. I used to try to draw her out of her retreat, get her to be sociable, but I realised eventually that she was really happier her way."

"Well, there are worse ways of spending Christmas than planting roses."

"Yes. When you don't depend on other people, it gives you a marvellous freedom, when you come to think of it."

"Your mother depended on one other person, heavily. I've never known a union so close as hers with David. Excluded the world. Rare."

"Yes," said Josephine, thinking that she had felt the

exclusion, too, without realising it. They had both loved her dearly, but she had been on the perimeter, as it were. But it had not mattered, because, although as an only child she could have been lonely, there was always Mike.

"This pheasant's delicious," said Hester. "I'm really beginning to enjoy my food again. Mike, that predatory young woman who was after you yesterday is making signals to you now. The table behind the trio."

Mike waved a hand in acknowledgment of Diana's signals, and said mildly,

"I thought it was only males who were predators in your book, Hester."

"There are a few female ones too."

"Well, you want equality."

And they were off, teasing, bantering, in the friendly, easy way they had with each other. Diana, however, was not the girl to be satisfied with a wave. She was partnered by a tall, bearded young man whom she took by the hand and guided round the room to their table as soon as coffee was being served and the trio had started playing a selction of Bing Crosby's songs.

"Can we join your party, Dr. Wexford?" she asked, smiling. "Jim and I are finding it a bit draughty over there."

"Hester's party, my dear, not mine, but I'm sure you're both very welcome."

And as they sang I'm Dreaming of a White Christmas, Diana cleverly inserted herself next to Mike and Josephine found herself talking to the bearded Jim, who owned a little shop near the quay which sold pottery and paintings by local artists. He was interested in archaeology and would have proved a pleasant enough companion, she thought, if he had not been trying to conceal a smouldering anger at Diana's flagrant desertion, for she devoted herself to Mike with gay enthusiasm for most of the evening, pulling him on to the dance floor at the first opportunity. Mike submitted with the same manner of easy indulgence that he had displayed the previous day, as though Diana was a pretty little kitten, amusing to play with. Jim dutifully danced with Josephine, whereat she discovered at least one of the reasons for Diana's defection, for Jim was heavy-footed with seemingly no ear for the beat of music, whereas Mike, as well she knew, was a comfortable and competent performer.

Hester was annoyed.

"Can you beat it for nerve? They learn young these days. She can't be a day older than nineteen. A mind as devoid of intelligence as those balloons, too. I tried to find something in it yesterday, but not a grain there. Have you hurt your ankle?"

Josephine stopped rubbing it.

"Jim's number elevens make themselves felt," she whispered, then rose with alacrity as Dr. Wexford indicated that he would like to waltz with her, for Jim was shuffling to his feet again.

"You're looking quite lovely tonight, dear. But, when nobody's looking, a little unhappy, I feel. Anything wrong?"

His eyes were kind and shrewd. A doctor's eyes, used to looking below the surface. With him, she could not prevaricate.

"My life is in a state of flux just now, and I seem to be unable to find a clear way ahead."

"You and Mike? That's all settled happily now?"

"We've buried the past with an amicable wreath. It

means nothing to Mike now, I'm sure, although I don't really know him these days," she added sadly.

"I'm sometimes a bit at sea myself. Those defences he put up - he can't seem to take them down. Bless my soul, that young man of Diana's has taken on Muriel, and he'll have her on the floor if he's not careful."

Fortunately for Josephine, a red-headed young man who told her he owned a fishing boat and knew the Wexfords, took a fancy to her and danced with her for most of the remainder of the evening, thus saving her from further damage from Jim and easing a little the hurt and humiliation of the fact that Mike did not dance once with her. As the last waltz was announced, her heart leapt as he came towards her, but it was to his aunt that he spoke.

"Come on, Aunt Muriel, display your skill at an old fashioned waltz. This is a nice dreamy one. You'll do it justice."

The thin cheeks of his aunt flushed with pleasure as she joined him, and they made one circle of the room alone, and to applause, for Miss Wexford, nearing seventy, was well known and popular in Mawnsey, where she was still active in local affairs. Watching them, Josephine was overpowered with longing to be in Mike's arms. She had known nothing like this urgency in the days of their engagement. Affection, liking, yes. But not this aching desire for him. A consciousness of his physical presence that seemed to burn in her blood. It was a completely new experience and it shattered her glib decision to put him out of her mind and heart. She was trembling as though she had a fever when she linked hands with the doctor and Hester as they stood in a circle for Auld Lang Syne.

The rain had stopped and Josephine was glad of the

cool, sweet air as they waited in the porch of the inn for Mike to bring the car round. He dropped his father and aunt at Tamarisk Cottage and then drove Hester and Josephine back to the farmhouse. He gave Hester an arm up the path. Over the door hung a bunch of mistletoe.

"Well, aren't you going to give us a fond good-night?" asked Hester, glancing up at it.

"Do my ears deceive me? An invitation to a male predator. Hester, you're slipping. Good-night, my dears," he added, giving Hester a friendly hug and striding back to the car.

"Well!" exclaimed Hester. "As neat a brush-off as ever I saw. His highness evidently feels too old for childish games, or perhaps he's had his fill of Diana this evening, and serve him right. If we weren't old friends, I'd take umbrage."

Upstairs alone in her room at last, Josephine sat down on the bed and despised herself for the tears she could not stem.

# 12

# A Helping Hand

She awoke sluggishly the next morning to the sound of rain beating on the window and a loud knocking on her door. It was Mrs. Rossland.

"There's a telephone call for you, Miss Riverton. It's urgent."

She tied her dressing-gown round her as she ran down the stairs to the hall, alarmed by the dismay on the kindly face of the farmer's wife. The call came from the Dilford general hospital. Her mother had been discovered unconscious in her garden by a neighbour, had been taken to the hospital but had died without regaining consciousness during the night. They had been unable to contact her before, as it had taken the neighbour some time to find her whereabouts from a letter Josephine had written to her mother and which had been left half hidden on a sideboard.

The rest of that day passed as a kind of nightmare, when she found herself talking and acting normally while underneath she felt stunned and cold with disbelief. She packed a case after trying to swallow a cup of coffee and some toast, and asked Hester if she could take her car.

"You're not fit to drive all that way. Mike will take you, I'm sure. He was returning tomorrow, anyway. A day earlier will make no difference."

"No. I don't want to bother him."

"My dear, if you can't turn to friends when you're in trouble, who can you turn to? In any case, you must break the news to them." She looked at Josephine's white face with concern. She was unnaturally calm. "I'll let them know. You get on with your packing," she said, limping out.

When she returned, she said,

"Dr. Wexford insists on going with you. Mike will drive."

During the long drive back, Dr. Wexford managed to break through the barrier which shock had erected and comfort her.

"She died in the garden she loved, without pain, unknowing. I had a word with the hospital after you phoned. A heart attack. She would have known nothing about it. If I could choose a way to go, that would be it."

"Yes," said Josephine, nodding blindly.

He took her hand, then put his arm round her as she laid her head on his shoulder and let the tears come. It was better so, he thought. She must weep for her own loss, but there was no need to weep on her mother's behalf. He had seen too much of the ravages of old age to wish to live beyond the span of an active life, and Joyce Riverton, of all people, would share his feeling. She had half died, anyway, when David went. She would be the last person to want to drag on, a burden to her daughter, unable to work in her garden. Josephine was young, with her own life to lead. The resilience of youth would see her through this bereavement. Her mother's love of solitude, though, meant that there were few friends to help her through the necessary formalities. And there were no close relatives. He would willingly take that burden from the shoulders of David's daughter, he thought, sighing as his thoughts turned to the past and a friendship that had meant much to him.

133

And so Dr. Wexford returned to Elmfield, staying at an inn a mile outside the village, and made all the funeral arrangements, aided by Mike. There were only a few local people at the funeral at the church in Elmfield, for her mother was little known. It crossed Josephine's mind to wonder what Mike was feeling on this, his first visit to Elmfield since her break with him and the subsequent gossip had driven him away. He remained grave and impassive. She could not read his thoughts at all.

She tried to express her gratitude to his father after it was all over. He brushed her thanks aside.

"The least I could do. I was very fond of your parents."

"After the way I hurt you and Mike—it was very generous of you," she said painfully.

"That, my dear, was not your fault. You must rid yourself of any sense of guilt."

"You're going back by train?"

"Yes. Mike's driving me to Paddington tomorrow morning. If you need any advice at any time, you have only to telephone, dear, or get in touch with Mike. But I shouldn't decide to do anything in a hurry. It will be lonely here on your own, though."

"Yes. I've loved the cottage, but somehow, without my mother. . . it was so much part of her. She always saw the garden as a memorial to my father. I may sell it and move to a flat."

"That would probably be a wise thing to do. You're too young to live with memories of the past."

Mike was kind, too, when he called in the next evening. She wondered whether his father had asked him to keep an eye on her, She made him coffee, but he did not stay long.

"If there's any way I can help, Jo, let me know."

"Yes. Thank you," she said, her eyes searching his face painfully. She wanted his arms round her, wanted him to comfort her with the warmth of love and affection in a world that had gone cold. But she could feel his constraint like a wound inside her.

"You know, what you need is a holiday. You've had a tiring time looking after Hester, and now this blow," he added, looking at her strained face. "Why not try to get away for a bit? You've nothing to keep you. Hester's on her feet again now."

She nodded and he rose to go.

"I've been sorting out books and papers today," she said. "In a box in Mother's room I found among other things a bundle of papers and maps and photographs all relating to a climbing holiday in the Alps which my father had with yours. I thought your father might like to have them. I'll fetch them, and perhaps you'd take them down next time you go to Cornwall."

"Sure. I'll fetch them," he said, waving her back to the chair, which she was making a great effort to quit. "Tell me where they are."

"I left them on the chest of drawers in my room, on the right at the top of the stairs."

She leaned back in the chair, exhausted with the strain of pent-up feelings, longing to throw herself in his arms, but resolved not to embarrass him by taking advantage of his kindness, which he had proffered, it was obvious, from a sense of duty and because he was sorry for her. She felt humiliated by her need for him in the face of his utter rejection of her on Boxing-night, a rejection that burned in her still. Her pride would come back, she thought, when she felt stronger, when time had healed the first shock of her mother's death. Meanwhile, she must hang on. She heard his footsteps overhead, and closed her eyes, wishing him gone before she gave way. She need not have worried. He looked in, with the papers in his hand, and said briefly,

"I'll be off, Jo. Thanks for these. My father will get a good deal of nostalgic pleasure from them. Don't bother to come to the door."

A minute later, she heard his car drive off.

\* \* \*

The New Year came in with typically spiteful weather, a mixture of east winds, rain and sleet, which gave Hester impetus for her plan. Josephine, calling in for tea one wet afternoon in mid-January, found her friend in ebullient mood.

"I've had a brilliant idea, Jo. No fewer than five of my friends, and I make the sixth, are in need of a holiday to buck them up, and it occurred to me today, after talking to Nick on the phone, that it would be a splendid idea to get together and escape from this dreary weather to the sun for a couple of weeks. It would be better still to go for a couple of months, of course, but one has to be practical, since we're all working people."

"Sounds a good plan to me. Who are the needy?"

"You, for one. You've had a rotten time and look as wan as a ghost. Nick's just had 'flu and was cursing the climate in that elegant way of his. Jean Brynton is going to have a baby in July. They're delighted, and Darrel would like to get her away for a holiday in the sun to give her a pick-me-up before the infant makes itself felt. Guy tells me Mike's working much too hard and needs a break, and that accident I had has left me a bit under par, too, to say nothing of the fact that I always feel washed up when I've just finished a book. Now what do you say to trying to arrange for the six of us to take a winter break in the south of France? I know an excellent hotel at Menton, a place to suit all tastes at this time of the year."

Josephine sipped her tea and thought about it. She had recovered from the shock of her mother's death, but found herself in a state of unhappy inertia. The thought of an escape to the sun lifted her spirits, although she was sure that one member of the proposed party would find an excuse not to join them when he knew that she would be one of the party. She kept this to herself, however, and said,

"I think it's a lovely idea. Count me in. What sort of a place is Menton?"

"Interesting little town, especially the old part. Nice promenade, lovely walks in the foothills behind for the likes of you country-lovers, and lots of cafés to linger in and watch the world go by for the likes of urban types like me. And at this time of the year, a spring-like climate."

"Say no more. You've sold it to me."

"Good. I'll telephone Nick right away. I'm sure he'll fall in if he hasn't got any urgent literary projects or functions on hand."

He hadn't and welcomed the suggestion. Hester, always an energetic planner, then telephoned Jean, and got a qualified acceptance pending a consultation with Darrel that evening.

"That leaves Mike," said Hester, glancing at the clock. "He'll not be home yet. I'll pop down to his flat about six. Hope he'll agree, and balance the party. Five's an odd number."

Not a hope, thought Josephine, still smarting from the

Boxing-night humiliation. If he could so deliberately avoid having one dance with her and even snub Hester as well to escape a light-hearted kiss under the mistletoe at Christmas, he would cetainly not join a party which included her for a whole fortnight. It was more than a lack of interest. It was a positive aversion.

"I wonder who else might come if you can't get Mike," she said.

"Any unattached male you'd like?"

"Can't think of one at the moment. I lost touch when I left Conrad."

"In any case, it needs to be someone we all know and like. We six are old friends, and can be quite easy together and go our own ways and do our own thing if we want to. No, it must be Mike. I'll work on him."

Hester went on to enthuse about Menton and that part of the coast bordering on Italy, fetching a map and a guide to show to Josephine. Soon after six, she went down to Mike's flat and was gone for some time. To Josephine's surprise, she came back with a partial victory.

"He thinks he might be able to manage a week, but leaves me to fix the dates with the rest and let him know. He'll fit in if and when he can, because he's got a court case at the end of the month."

"Don't count your chickens. Did he seem enthusiastic?" asked Josephine, trying to keep the irony out of her voice.

"Not madly, but he's only just got home and looked very tired. Guy's right. He's working too hard. If I look in on him, he's usually got papers strewn all over his desk. Either that, or he's listening to music. So in any case, I don't feel I can linger. And when he goes off to Cornwall, he's usually got a fat brief-case with him."

138

"Doesn't sound as though he has much time for his glamorous actress."

"Penelope Rockdale? I asked him about her one day, but of course got little from him. He'd known her for some years, he said. A good friend. And that was that. Mike and I get on very well, as you know. As friendly and easy together as kiss your hand, but anything remotely touching his personal life and he closes up like an oyster. I wonder what put those bars up so securely. Not that I particularly like people who spill their all over you at the drop of a hat, but Mike intrigues me."

"You just like to know what makes people tick," said Josephine, smiling.

"Well, the writer's approach, I guess. Mind you, Nick's the same, but with an entirely different method of defence. Witty, urbane, he smiles your probing away with such exquisite courtesy and gentle mockery that you go away empty-handed thinking what a delightful person he is, having learned absolutely nothing. I've known Nick for a long time and love him dearly, but he remains essentially an enigma. He does it with charm, Mike with reserve. But behind Mike, you can sense the passion. Behind Nick, just a question mark."

"Well, I guess we all have our private rooms."

"And I'm just a curious novelist, picking people over. Perhaps that's why they feel they need defences. Do *you* know what goes on behind that powerful character downstairs? After all, you knew him when you were children, didn't you?"

"Yes. Our families were friends. But he's changed a lot since then. He's almost a stranger to me now. But he and his father have been very kind to me these past weeks, for old times' sake. Dr. Wexford and my father were very close friends," added Josephine, and steered the conversation away from Mike by asking more questions about Menton and the best way to get there.

Driving back to the empty cottage that night, she found herself looking forward to this unexpected escape from the loneliness of her home and the wretched weather which seemed to match her spirits just then. She felt certain in her own mind that Mike would find it impossible to join them, after all. Work was always a valid excuse. But she was fond of Hester and had a warm feeling for the Bryntons and Nick Barbury, and would enjoy a holiday in their company. Never again, she thought fiercely, would she approach Mike. One slap in the face was enough. But she wondered when it would stop hurting.

Wrenching her thoughts from him, she smiled to herself at Hester's liking to assemble people in a fresh setting to stimulate her mind again, once her book was finished. While she was writing, she was obsessed with her characters, all living people were intruders, and she liked a hermit's life. The book finished, she was conscious of a vacuum which needed to be filled with new outside stimulants, and now, busy and energetic as a bee, she was organising this expedition to that end. And as far as Josephine was concerned, she was very pleased that it should be so.

# 13

# *Menton*

In the space of the next few days, Hester had it all worked out. She telephoned Josephine with details.

"Nick, you and I will fly out on the twenty-ninth. Jean doesn't want to fly, and she and Darrel are going to travel by train from Dieppe. They're planning to stop in Paris for a couple of nights on the way and will join us after that. Mike will come for the second week. Can't get away before. So it's worked out pretty well. I'm going to see to all the hotel bookings."

"Splendid. Something to look forward to. Thank you for being such a good shepherd," said Josephine.

"My pleasure. By the way, I've just read your article in the magazine. 'Remembered Paths of Summer.' Jo, it's a lovely piece of writing. You hide your light under a bushel, you know. Haven't been so thrilled with a piece of writing for a long time."

"Glad you like it."

"I should say so. A long way above the usual provincial standard, if you ask me. Real quality. Nothing banal. A sensitive Chekov-like looking back with love and regret. I'm cutting it out to show Nick. Real talent there. Mind you serve it instead of looking after old hacks like me. Be seeing you."

She had rung off before Josephine could say anything more, but her friend's generous praise had warmed the day for her, knowing as she did that Hester was never anything but brutally honest where her views of writing were concerned, and that she knew what she was talking about. Josephine had put her heart into that piece of writing, and had had to use a blue pencil afterwards to cut parts where she felt her emotions had been too intrusive.

The desultory writing she had done since her mother's death had not satisfied her, for the desired concentration was lacking, pushed out by thoughts of her mother and Mike and the whole sad disarray of her personal life. She still did not believe that Mike would join them. Some last minute excuse would be found. Or did he think that there would be safety in numbers? That there would be no difficulty in keeping a distance between them in the company of the other four? He need not worry. She would help him there, she thought bitterly. And there could be no pleasanter companion for solace than Nick Barbury.

*     *     *

To their surprise and disappointment, their first few days in Menton were unremittingly wet, with heavy black clouds massing over the mountain tops behind the little town. Hester and Nick chose to sit it out in their very comfortable hotel, but Josephine enjoyed exploring the town and surroundings, rain or not, enchanted by the broad boulevards lined with orange trees, the gay little shops with their bright awnings, the market, and, above all, by the old town on the hill, with its long flights of steps mounting between the white walls of the old houses, leading to the baroque church and the pebbled Italianate square in front of it. The tiny gardens, for on that hill space was limited, were bright with mimosa trees in bloom, aloes, bougainvillaea tumbling down walls and the orange trees seen everywhere in Menton, the ripe fruit glowing in golden abundance so that even in the rain, the effect was rich and colourful.

During those solitary explorations, she threw off her personal problems, resolutely living only in the present, responding to the tonic of fresh scenes, a different environment. And then, on the third day, when they went to the station to meet Jean and Darrel, the clouds rolled back and the sun appeared, and it was a gay party that assembled for dinner that evening. Jean, heart-warmingly happy, talked about the magic of Paris, and she and Darrel, in no way tired by the long train journey, insisted on strolling out with them after dinner along the promenade, with the dark Mediterranean in a calm mood on one side of them, and the lights of Menton making a magic pattern on the other and dying away in a sprinkling of starry lights up the slopes of the foothills behind.

It was a mild and lovely night, and they were all happy and at ease together. It was a long time since Josephine had felt so relaxed. Would she find her nerves tightening, tension creeping in, with Mike's arrival? Or would this enchanting little town, nestling in the foothills of the Alps, with its protective arc of mountain peaks guarding it from the north winds, cast a benign spell that would embrace Mike as well? She would not trouble him. Would see that they were not alone together. Would enjoy Nick's company. And meanwhile, put Mike out of her mind.

But this, simple to say, was, she found, difficult to achieve, for the party was a little unbalanced. Jean and Darrel went off on expeditions to the many botanical gardens in the area and explored the flora of the surroundings, an occupation of absorbing interest to horticultural experts but holding little appeal for Nick and Hester, who preferred poking round the town, sitting in cafés drinking coffee or apéritifs, and generally taking life easily, while Josephine longed to take a picnic lunch and walk in the foothills that looked so inviting, but did not wish to appear unsociable. If Mike were here, she thought, and it was like the old days, they would have been off exploring those hills on their feet every day. Nick, no walker, was missing his car and decided to hire one, a decision that held little appeal for Josephine, who viewed the panache of French drivers with apprehension, since the roads were narrow, busy and twisting, and motoring had only ever been a convenience to her and not a pleasure.

"But you can't see the country if you're driving, Nick," she said. "The roads are far too dangerous not to demand full concentration. Why not use the bus service? It's a very good one."

"Like to be able to please myself," said Nick lazily, eyeing her with approval.

They were sitting outside a little café in the town, drinking coffee. Hester had gone in search of an English newspaper, and the Bryntons had gone to Monaco for the day to investigate some exotic garden there. It was pleasantly warm, and Nick, lounging back with his usual air of detached elegance, was looking his handsome best in a smooth, light tweed suit, with a bizarre patterned tie in shades of pink, violet and grey. Not for Nick the jeans-and-pullover leisure wear favoured by his compatriots. Nick made his own rules. It was evident, however, that he approved of her trim navy blue trouser suit and red and white shirt, which was gratifying in view of his fastidious taste. As though sensing her thoughts, he said with a smile,

"You're one of the few females I know who look really

good in trousers. The right length of leg and slender hips. And you're the only one I know who blushes. Very old fashioned. And nice," he added.

She smiled at him. A shaft of sunlight across his hair lightened it to the colour of ripe wheat. She envied the cool detachment with which he viewed the world. She could not imagine those classical features disturbed by any deep emotion, by anger or passion or fear. And yet she knew that a shrewd and lively mind lived behind those apparently lazy eyes. She remembered Hester's observation. Behind Nick, a question mark. A private man.

"By the way," he went on, "congratulations, too, on that article you wrote. 'Remembered Paths of Summer.' Very choice. I'd have thought you were too young to convey nostalgia with such deep feeling. You ought to come to London, Jo. You've real talent. I could find you an opening that would give it scope, I'm sure."

"I don't like urban living."

"Think about it. Even a few years on the staff of a quality magazine would be good experience, allow your talent to grow. Hullo, Hester. Any luck?" he asked as Hester joined them.

"Yesterday's *Times*. I'll split it with you over coffee."

"Well, I'll leave you two sluggards to brood over the news," said Josephine, rising. "I've not come all the way to the Côte d'Azur to sit and read an English newspaper."

"Such energy," drawled Nick, lifting a languid hand in farewell.

If she wished to use Nick as a refuge from Mike, she thought, she would be leading a very static life, which was not her style at all. Perhaps she would have to play a lone hand, after all. She made her way back to the old town and climbed the steps and explored the winding streets and arched passages which held such charm for her. From a vantage point half way up, she could look down across a small paved garden full of Provençal pots containing aloes and palms to a fine view of the coast round the bay, bounded by the range of mountains which marked the boundary of Italy.

She sat on a coping, the sun warm on her face, and wished Mike was there to share it with her. What had happened to them, she wondered sadly, that they, who shared so many interests and tastes, could now no longer communicate? Why did Mike now find friendship with her impossible? Had she changed? Could he still not forget or forgive the horrible publicity Conrad had brought upon him? And what was she doing, she wondered angrily, pining for a man who had so plainly shown his aversion to her? Ever since that first traumatic meeting at Guy's house, he had shown as clearly as a man could show that he wanted nothing more to do with her, that he wanted to forget her. Where was her pride in not accepting that? She had rejected him once. Why did she still think in some deep recess of her heart that because she knew now that she loved him as she had never loved him before, he could still feel his old love for her? It was such a muddle, she thought. She could not see clearly. Could not penetrate Mike's defences to the man underneath. And deep down was an uneasy feeling that she had mishandled the whole affair.

She realised afterwards that a conversation which she had with Jean that evening might have helped her to see more clearly, but her mind seemed unable to see the wood for the trees until it was too late. They had strolled out after dinner to the gardens which their hotel overlooked. These were planted with orange trees, acacias and palms, tree-ferns and other exotic trees which Josephine could not identify. The flower-beds were full of cyclamen of many colours, and fountains played at each end and in the centre of the gardens. It was a cool, calm night, with a full moon rising above the mountain peaks, and the gardens made an oasis of mysterious charm, with the lights from the hotel twinkling down through the trees and the floodlit fountains standing out from the shadowy glades surrounding them.

They stood by the central rectangular pool. Jets of water danced along the two long sides, a fountain was centrally placed at each of the two short sides, and presiding over all stood the carved stone figure of a woman, one arm protectively round a child.

"I love these gardens," said Jean. "An atmosphere of happiness and peace here."

"How did you enjoy the botanic gardens in Monaco today?"

"Fascinating. But so many aloes and cacti and sea-urchins, all spiny things, are a bit overwhelming. There are warnings about touching the spikes, because many of them are poisonous. I really prefer my plants and flowers to be more kindly, and found these a bit sinister, but Darrel was keenly interested, of course."

"He was a wee bit annoyed this evening with Hester, I fancy, for taking you to task about giving up your job in the bookshop just because you're going to have a baby."

Jean laughed.

"She was really getting at him, implying that he was a male chauvinist, for she dearly likes to ride her women's-lib horse, but the decision was mine, not Darrel's."

"You're very happy about it, aren't you? The baby, I mean."

"Yes. We've been married six years. I was beginning to get a little worried, since we both want a family. A small one," she added with a smile.

"You'll miss the shop at first, I expect," said Josephine, who knew the little bookshop in Dilford which Jean ran with Nick's cousin, Alison, and had always thought it a very happy partnership.

"I shall keep in touch. Be handy for emergencies. But home and family come first. I suffered very much as a child from a career-orientated household. My mother was a famous opera singer whose career took her all over the world, and my father was a scientist absolutely wrapped up in research. I wouldn't want our children to have a home where they felt an irrelevant nuisance, as I did."

"You have a point there. What was your mother's name? I'm an opera lover myself."

"Thea Lansford."

"I've heard records. So that's why you and Mike were able to guy opera so beautifully at Guy's house-warming party that night."

"Fancy remembering that," said Jean, smiling. "Mike would have a good voice if it was trained."

They had sat down on a seat near the pool, and Josephine said,

"It's good to see you and Darrel so happy and making a success of marriage to confound Hester's scepticism. You two seem to make it look so easy, and yet I wouldn't have said that Darrel was the easiest of propositions, much as I like him. A shade domineering, would you say?" added Josephine with a twinkle in her eyes.

"You could say that. We understand each other. I've been tremendously fortunate. We had our troubles before we married, you know. All my fault."

"I can't imagine that."

"True. I was once engaged to Darrel's cousin, Adrian. A few weeks before our wedding, we were involved in a disaster at sea. A fire. No need to go into details, but when our lives were in danger, Adrian forgot me in saving a girl I'd thought a mere acquaintance. I fought to reach him in a panic-stricken crowd, and he shrugged me off in his concern to protect the girl I afterwards discovered he loved. It all ended tragically. Adrian was killed in a car accident in Ireland a week or two later. The girl was Irish and her family and religion had kept them apart. And that rejection coming on top of the rejection I'd always felt by my parents had a devastating effect on me and nearly wrecked the chance of happiness Darrel offered me. I'd lost all confidence in myself. All judgment. I just couldn't believe that he really loved and wanted me."

"But what followed made up for all that had gone before," said Josephine gently, surprised by these revelations, for nothing about Jean suggested past tragedy.

"More than that. But I can still shudder at the recollection of how nearly I threw it all away. I owe Darrel so much. He restored my confidence in myself. When you've been rejected by someone you love, you need a terrible lot of reassuring afterwards. It damages, you, somehow. You lose trust. And that's why I don't intend that our children shall be handicapped by any feeling of rejection," she concluded lightly, as though fearing she had been too solemn.

"I can see how absolutely right Darrel is for you. Nobody could doubt the strength of his support. Or feel they didn't belong for keeps," said Josephine with a little smile which Jean did not see as Darrel loomed up behind them.

"Thought you might want this," he observed, draping a coat round Jean's shoulders. "Mediterranean nights aren't exactly balmy at this time of the year."

Jean, who only had a light jacket over her thin dress, accepted the coat and patted the seat beside her.

"Come and contemplate the fountains with us. So restful after all those vindictive plants we saw today."

Darrel put his arm round Jean's shoulders.

"We'll take it easy tomorrow. Catch a bus into the hills to Gorbio, perhaps. It's a pretty village, I believe. Just potter. Suit you?"

"I potter round the village and sit over coffee in a café, while you potter in the hills after rare botanic specimens, scaling a few peaks at the same time, you mean?"

"I am yours to command," said Darrel, rubbing the nape of his wife's neck with a gentle, admonishing finger.

"You've made me into quite a keen plant-hunter myself," said Jean demurely, "and in spite of Hester, I'm not a sit-at-home little woman while you have all the fun, as you well know."

"To my great benefit," said Darrell gallantly. "I know I shall be reprimanded if I suggest that I don't want you to over-tire yourself. . . "

"So you won't say it," interjected Jean, laughing.

Josephine left them on the seat and walked through the town to the sea. After six years of marriage, it was obvious that the Bryntons were as close as they could ever have been. It was warming to see two people find such fulfilment in each other. And then, like a terrier with a bone, her thoughts returned to Mike, due the next day, worrying again at the painful barrier between them.

# 14

# The Lost Key

Nick, having hired a car, drove Hester to Nice Airport to meet Mike. When Hester asked Josephine if she was coming, she declined.

"Best leave the back of the car for Mike and his luggage. I thought of walking round Cap Martin today to Roquebrune. See you for dinner."

And so she spent the day walking along the winding path half way between the sea and the top of the cliff, with the warmth of the sun bringing out the rich scents of the aromatic shrubs and trees. She loved the heady scent of maquis country, which she remembered from her travels in France with Conrad, and had forgotten until now. As she walked along, she recognised lavender and sage, and a yellow jasmine, myrtle trees and olives, and numerous parasol pines through which she could see the cobalt blue sea below. From the point of the peninsula, she looked back at a fine view of Menton and its surrounding mountains, the highest peaks bearing a sprinkling of snow.

She took it easily, needing this quiet day on her own to prepare for her meeting with Mike. Remembering his deliberate avoidance of her, she had decided to play it coolly, friendly but detached, unless she saw any change of heart on his part, and she couldn't think why there should be. She at least owed it to him, in view of all that had happened in the past, to avoid embarrassing him and spoiling his holiday by seeking him out.

Just short of Roquebrune, she came on a seat overlooking a rocky inlet, where she took out her picnic lunch of good French bread, cheese, a banana and an orange, and sunned herself, wishing that her mind was as tranquil as the scene about her. Afterwards she explored the village, and climbed to the castle before returning to Menton by the same footpath round the cape. Tired by her efforts, she soaked in a hot bath to fortify herself for the evening. When she went down to dinner, she was annoyed to find herself trembling with nervous tension.

Her eyes, as though drawn by a magnet, found him immediately. They were in the lounge, sitting in a circle of armchairs, waiting for her. Mike was leaning back in his chair, long legs stretched before him, smiling at something Nick was saying. He stood up as she joined them. To hide her nervous state, she summoned up the social poise of her Conrad days and said with a smile,

"Hullo, Mike. Welcome to the Côte d'Azur. Hope you had a good flight."

His dark blue eyes met hers intently, then he said pleasantly,

"Very good, thanks. It was snowing when I left Heathrow. Good to see the sun when I arrived this afternoon."

They all had a lot to tell him about Menton over dinner, and Josephine chatted as happily as any of them with no hint of the tight little knot of tension inside her. They sat over coffee in the lounge afterwards until Mike said,

"I'd like to have a look round Menton. It's a fine night. Any offers?"

"After that dinner? Not on your life," drawled Nick.

There was a lack of enthusiasm on all sides, for Darrel and Jean's day of pottering in the hills had, as Jean had expected, turned into quite an arduous exercise, and Hester would only ever turn out at night for entertainment.

152

"What about you, Jo? Care to show me around?"

It was the first time he had asked for her company since their paths had crossed again. It was spoken casually, and he was probably just being polite, as she was the only person present who had not given a definite refusal. Remembering the brush-off at Christmas, she smiled regretfully as she said,

"I've walked my feet off today, Mike, and I'm challenging Nick to a nice restful game of Scrabble tonight after he beat me hollow last night."

"It's on," said Nick.

"Why don't you leave the explorations until tomorrow, Mike, and relax? You look a bit tired," said Hester.

"Been sitting about all day. Need some fresh air." He glanced round their little circle, then added, "It's good to see you all looking so well."

"And it's good to have you with us," said Hester.

"He smiled, saluted them and left. Josephine's eyes followed him across the lounge. Had she done the right thing, not imposing herself on him, or had she rejected a chance of narrowing the yawning gap between them? There had been something in his eyes. A question? There she went again, dithering and uneasy. What was wrong with her that she could not think clearly, act decisively?

During the next few days, half by accident, half by design, she found herself spending most of her time with Nick, motoring along the twisting corniches with their magnificent views of the coast, visiting museums and lingering in cafés. Hester declared that Nick's driving along those steep, narrow and twisting roads matched the panache of the natives and gave her nerves no rest, apart from which she suffered from vertigo over the high passes, while the Bryntons and Mike preferred to explore on their feet. Josephine's nerves were tried a little on the hair-pins, too, but in fact Nick was a skilled driver, and she had confidence in him. If her thoughts were nearly all the time with Mike in spite of trying to school herself, she found Nick's company very pleasant and they both enjoyed talking literary shop.

It was when they were sitting on a seat in the gardens by the hotel late one afternoon after a day out in Monaco that he mentioned her article again.

"It struck right home, Jo. Like some passages of music. Heart-ache and regret for the passing of summer days. Straight through the chinks in the armour we all wear. It really got through a hardened old type like me."

"You're not hard, Nick. You're an unusually tolerant and kind person. You don't wear armour, just an elegant cloak. You do seem to glide through life easily, though. A loner. Have you never lost your heart, been unhappy? Had your citadel threatened?"

"Once, long, long ago."

"What happened?"

"Abortive. The lady loved another. Just as well. We both had a lucky escape, I guess. Now I lose my heart to the works of writers and poets and composers, if I lose it at all. Much safer. And infinitely rewarding."

"But, at the end of the day, a little lonely, perhaps?"

He eyed her quizzically.

"You wouldn't be suggesting that it's a good policy to endure an uncongenial job all your life for the sake of the pension at the end, would you?"

"I wouldn't attempt to recommend any change of life-style to you, Nick," she said, laughing, "when your own so obviously suits you to a degree that we all might envy."

He put an arm round her shoulders as he replied,

"Who knows, when you start peeling away the layers, what you'll find underneath? You, I think, dear Jo, are floundering a little now. Your mother's death? Or troubles of another kind?"

"Shall we say I'm in a tangled wood just now. Can't see ahead."

"I'm good at listening, and very discreet."

"I know. You would be my first choice for advice, I think, if I didn't know that this is something I have to work out myself. But...thanks, Nick. You don't know what a boon your calm detachment is. Like a cool drink on a hot day."

"Come to London. Concentrate on journalism. Work that you like offers the most rewards, you know. And I shall enjoy providing cool drinks."

"I'll think about it," she said, smiling, and he drew her closer, settling himself down as though intending to stay there contemplating the fountains for the rest of time. And it was at this point that Mike and Hester appeared along the path by the pool.

"Hullo, there," said Hester. "You two look very comfortable."

"We are," said Nick blandly. "Come and join us in contemplation. These fountains are hypnotic."

Since Nick did not move and still held Josephine within one arm, and they occupied the middle of the seat, Hester plumped down on the other side of Nick and Mike sat next to Josephine. She had flushed when his dark eyes had studied her, and now every fibre burned with consciousness of his nearness. He was wearing a thin light blue polo-necked sweater with navy slacks and windcheater. Clothes always sat well on him, she thought, even the charmless rough-weather sailing gear of oilskins.

He was well built, everything in proportion, lean, and a lithe mover. His shoulder brushed hers, and that little knot of tension made itself felt again. If Nick was like a cool drink, Mike acted on her like a mouthful of too-hot curry.

"And how did you like Monaco?" he asked.

"A fairy-tale place. The palace, the setting, the old town, all pure magic. You must go," added Josephine, nerves making her talk too quickly. "You'll be fascinated by the old town, Mike. Little alleys, all paved, quiet, with no traffic. The law-court building reminded me of a Merchant of Venice setting. Lovely. In brown stone with double sweeping staircases outside. The little houses are built of a lovely gold, almost ochre-coloured, stone, and wherever there's a tiny space, there's a courtyard with Provençal pots of greenery or a small tree. And. . ." She stopped, conscious that she was sounding like a guide-book.

"You'll gather that it's a desirable place to visit," said Nick. "Amazing that all we got from Darrel and Jean after their visit was that sinister picture of prickly plants. And what have you two been doing?"

"Went on the bus to Nice. Had a very enjoyable day, and were making a bee line from the bus stop to the nearest *salon de thé* when your blissful images diverted us. I simply cannot resist those dreamy *pâtisseries,* although the price has me reeling."

"Good idea," said Nick. "Let's go."

Walking back to the hotel after tea, Josephine found herself beside Mike, well behind Hester and Nick.

"Haven't seen much of you this holiday, Jo. You've enjoyed it, I can see."

"Immensely. The time's flying by. Only two more clear days. A pity you could only manage a week, but you missed the wet spell we started off with."

"By the way, just before I came away I met that boy you took to the cricket match. Barry. Couldn't place him at first. Met him in Fordingham High Street, coming out of a sports shop. It was his birthday, and his father had just bought him a new cricket bat. He came up to show it to me. I was amazed that he remembered me."

"Barry always remembers people who have been kind to him because he's experienced so much of the reverse, and kindness has been a bit thin on his ground. Things have improved for him now, though, I think. That was his newly-acquired stepfather you saw."

"How did you get to know him?"

She told him, glad of a fairly safe topic of conversation, even if the mention of Conrad's household raised unpleasant memories.

"Barry will have to get the county captain's autograph again now. It was kind of you to go to so much trouble that day," she concluded awkwardly.

"You always did have a soft heart for underdogs, Jo."

She stopped at the window of a shop close to the hotel which displayed a little picture she had fallen in love with.

"I have to stop and look at it every time I go by," she explained. "That little girl's face has captivated me, to say nothing of the spaniel."

Mike studied the picture. It was a very small reproduction of a Reynolds' painting set in a deep black and gold frame. The child's heart-shaped face framed with straight chestnut hair looked out with grave brown eyes that seemed to hold a secret which she was determined to keep from the world. She was clasping a black and white spaniel round his neck, and the dog, too, sprawling comfortably in her embrace, looked out with the same secret air of contentment which needed to be guarded from the world.

"It's charming. An unusual reproduction. A process I've not seen before. It preserves the colour and line marvellously."

"It's called *Miss Bowles*. They live in an enchanted private world of their own, those two. I'd love to have it, but the price is too much for my holiday allowance, I'm afraid."

They walked on, and he took her arm to hold her back as she went to cross the road to the hotel and was threatened by a motorist sweeping round a corner. She wondered if he felt her trembling as they crossed arm-in-arm.

"I can't get used to the traffic being on the right instead of the left-hand side," she said hurriedly as she preceded him into the hotel.

In her room, she stood by the window looking down as the lights came on round the gardens, and wondered miserably why she could not break through this constraint with Mike. Dogged by his aloofness with her over Christmas, and, indeed, ever since she had told him the truth about Conrad's cruel part in their separation, she seemed now unable to behave naturally with him at all. Since his arrival, she had once or twice thought that there was a change in his attitude. She had kept her distance, but when they had been together, he had been affable enough, and she had several times caught him studying her intently, his face difficult to read, but sometimes she thought she caught a hint of that same deep pain that she had glimpsed once before. Looking back at that old easy friendship of her youth, it was impossible to understand the constrained, puzzling relationship between them now.

Once, Mike had been so easy to understand. The volatile, frank young man with the low flash-point, a fiery temper that rocketed up and died down as swiftly, and a sense of humour that was on the same wave-length as hers. Now he kept an iron control over those emotions. She sensed the passion there, but it was disciplined now, the Cornish blood mastered by the cooler English side of him, for Dr. Wexford always maintained that Cornwall was a separate nation.

The real trouble, perhaps, was the length of time that had elapsed since that disastrous break with him. Had she discovered the truth and been able to remove some of the bitterness soon after the break, he would not have become a stranger to her. But the gap had been too long. Feelings had hardened. The wound had healed and calloused over, and feelings had been calloused over, too. And all the time, she felt that there was a key, but she could not find it. Could only behave unnaturally with him, the victim of some paralysing nervous constraint.

# 15

# *Explosion*

Josephine had arranged to go back to Monaco with Nick the next morning to take some photographs of the old town, for she had run out of film the previous day, but Nick suggested a change of plan.

"Jean, Darrel and Hester want to go across the border into Italy and visit San Remo. Hester's willing to trust my driving, as other means of communication are not all that convenient. What about it? Can squeeze in a fifth. Mike's opted out. He's set to walk round Cap Martin."

She hesitated. Five people would be quite a crush in the little car Nick had hired.

"I'll stick to my plan, I think, Nick. I can get a bus into Monaco easily enough. I don't want to miss getting those photographs, and the weather might go back on us tomorrow."

"Sure?"

"Sure."

And so she spent the morning in Monaco, photographing the old houses with their wrought-iron balconies and pots of geraniums and tumbling bougain-villaea, the stone archways and tiny shops, the fairy-tale palace and the splendid cathedral. She enjoyed the day, away from the pressures of other people, fond as she was of her friends. After a light lunch in a café close to the harbour, where many expensive yachts were moored, waiting for the summer season, she caught the bus back, and, on impulse, got off short of Menton to walk back round Cap Martin, for it was the same bright, spring-like weather which they had enjoyed for the past week and she wanted to make the most of it. And perhaps she would see Mike on the way and manage to ease the constraint between them on the walk back to Menton.

She saw him ahead of her about half way back. He was sitting on a fallen tree trunk, gazing at the sea across a tangled growth of shrubs and parasol pine trees. Her crêpe-soled shoes made little sound on the path against the wash of the sea, and as she drew near him, it was a grim profile that came clear. He looked lost in some deep, painful reflection. She summoned up a lightness of approach.

"Hullo, Mike. Wondered if I might meet you on my way back. Can I join you for a breather?"

He looked surprised to see her, and the mask came down over his face. She sensed that he was in a dark mood, but he said affably enough,

"Sure. You didn't go with the others to San Remo, then."

"No. I had a day alone with my camera in Monaco."

"Communal holidays can be a little wearing," he said laconically, and she wondered, not for the first time, why he had joined them, knowing her to be one of the party.

"I've enjoyed it. A part of the Riviera I'd never visited. Much the nicest part," she said.

"You miss that side of your job with Ravensburg, perhaps."

"No. But I did enjoy the opportunities to travel. I wouldn't have missed them," she added in a nervy spurt of defiance.

There was silence between them for several moments, then he said coolly,

"Have you decided whether to sell your cottage?"

"Yes. It's a lonely, sad place now. For my mother, it was a place where she still felt the presence of my father. Now, it seems haunted by both of them. I'm putting it on the market when I get back."

"I think you're wise. Any plans about where you'll live?"

"Nothing definite."

"Nick and Hester think your best move to further your career would be to London."

"I'm not a city person."

"You would get used to it, I dare say. Nick would be there to help you."

His cold, dispassionate words fell on her heart like drops of icy water. Had her nerves not been in such a tense, strained state, she would have left it at that and walked on. But, fatally, her unhappiness expressed itself in irrational anger as she turned on him.

"You know I would never get used to it, and Nick is quite irrelevant to the question of where I live."

His eyebrows went up and he said with a cold irony that stung her,

"Sorry if I got the wrong impression."

"You did," she snapped.

"Why the bad temper?"

"Because I'm sick of being treated like an unwelcome stranger."

"*You* say that to *me*," he said incredulously, his eyes taking on a dangerous sparkle.

"Yes. I say that to you. You avoided me at Christmas as though I was infectious, you've made it plain that my efforts to be friends are not appreciated, and yet you join a holiday party that includes me. Why, if I'm so hateful to you? After all the years our families have known each other, your attitude is cruel and unreasonable. I suppose your pride can't forgive or forget."

He was looking at her in angry amazement, his face white under the tan, his mouth as grim as an arctic winter. Recklessly, she did not care. She wanted to break down that implacable defence, make him reveal his feelings, whatever they were.

"You don't understand," he said savagely. "You never did understand, and you never will. You want me to trot round you like some tame dog, wagging my tail, so that you can pat my head and feel relieved that we're good little pals again. So that you needn't feel guilty about the past."

"I've no reason to feel guilty," she flashed. "It wasn't my fault that it happened as it did."

"Granted. But you did feel guilty, all the same. It's been in your eyes every time you look at me. It's the reason for your pathetic efforts to be friends, as you term it in your infantile way. Please, I didn't mean it to be like that, you say with every gesture, every placatory smile. It drives me mad."

"Would you rather I said I'm glad Conrad did what he did? That it served you right," she cried, as furious as he was now.

"You miss the whole point," he said, banging his fist on his thigh. "You're incapable of understanding."

"How should I understand when all your attitude has said is 'Keep off'."

"You should understand because you're a woman, not a teenager. When I first met you again, I thought you'd grown up, in a sophisticated way I didn't much care for, but I've realised since that underneath the Ravensburg gloss, you're still a child, wanting playmates, not liking any trouble. A happy little band of friends, to please you and amuse you, like Nick. Well, I'm not made to be a playmate for you."

"Then why did you come on this holiday to spoil the harmony?"

"To spoil your idea of harmony, you mean. The rest of us have got on harmoniously enough, but you want it all ways, don't you, Jo? To be polite to you is not enough. You must feel that you have my friendship, otherwise you feel guilty and uncomfortable."

"You haven't answered my question. Why did you come, when you dislike being with me so much?"

"I came for two foolish reasons which have turned out to be quite mistaken. I think you'd do well to carry on your walk back alone now. I don't want to be brutal, but you've driven me beyond the bounds of control this time, Jo, and you've lost your temper, too. Just call it a day before more damage is done."

"No." she declared passionately. "I won't. I won't be treated like a stranger. Just come out with it. Say that you can't bear the sight of me, and never will be able to, and I'll know where I stand, and I'll see that you don't suffer any more," she concluded with such venom that she could hardly believe it was her voice that was saying the words.

He seized her by the shoulders in a grip that hurt, and his eyes searched her face with an intensity that was searing. But he had gained control over the fury that had threatened to erupt into violence, for he released her and leaned away from her, propping his weight on his arms behind him. Then he said quietly,

"What do you want of me, Jo?"

She stood up and gazed across the sea with unseeing

eyes, still shaken by anger at the cruel sarcasm of his criticism, unable to answer him. The gentle wash of the waves below was the only sound on that still day. She felt him get up and her body tensed. When she turned, he was leaning against a rocky outcrop a few feet away, still watching her with that same intensity. His next words took her completely by surprise, for he said quietly again,

"Kiss me, Jo."

As she stared at him, unable to move, and the seconds ticked way, an ironic, dismissive little smile curved his lips, and he turned and walked off without another word. And watching him go, she knew with absolute certainty that he was walking out of her life for ever. A strange paralysis gripped her until her legs refused to support her any longer, and she sat down on the tree trunk and put her head in her hands.

She did not move until the swift fall in temperature as it grew dark made her aware of the time. Walking back, all she could hear were his contemptuous words, infantile, playmates, incapable of understanding. And beneath her wincing anger lay an unbearable desolation at the finality of his departure.

If she had needed confirmation of that finality, she had it that same evening, in a form that surprised her but added even more to her desolation than any further angry exchanges would have done. She had slipped out after dinner to walk round the gardens, exhausted by the effort to appear natural and light-hearted with the others, to meet Mike's polite mask with equanimity. He must have noticed and followed her, for he caught up with her by the pool.

"Jo, I'm sorry I let go this afternoon. Forget it, will you? You've had a rotten time lately, and I don't want to spoil the last bit of the holiday for you. I know you mean well, and it was foolish of me to blame you for what you can't help. One day, when you fall in love with a man, you may look back and understand a bit better. Now just put it out of your mind, will you?"

He spoke lightly, kindly, as though to a child he had scolded too harshly. But put it out of her mind she never could.

"I let fly, too. We're quits."

"No hard feelings, then?"

"No."

"We're all so concerned to make the most of the last day that tomorrow's plans are a bit difficult to harmonise. Anyway, it's settled now that Darrel and I have a day in the hills, while Nick drives Jean to Nice, which she hasn't seen yet. What's your choice?"

"I haven't decided yet," she said lightly. "So many lovely places at hand, it's difficult to choose."

"Well, it's a good idea to wind up with the concert tomorrow evening. An attractive programme. Schubert and Debussy. Followed by a late supper at that little restaurant near the Casino. That's Hester's plan, anyway, and it sounds all right to me."

"Yes. I hope you'll have good weather for your day in the hills. There were some threatening clouds rolling up behind the mountains on the Italian side this evening."

"The hotel porter is reassuring. I'd better get back to study the map with Darrel. He likes to get everything organised. A bit chilly to linger. Coming?"

As they walked back towards the hotel together, chatting about the charms of Menton and its surroundings as though neither had a care in the world, Josephine thought what an incongruous way it was of saying

166

goodbye, for that, she knew, was what he was saying.

On their way they met Nick and Hester, setting out for a stroll round the town, which was gaily lighted and attractive by night. They had a drink on the waterfront in mind.

"What are your plans for tomorrow, Jo?" asked Hester. "A trip to Nice with Jean and Nick, toiling in the hills with the two male chauvinists, or pottering round the market and the old town with me? I've been gadding about so much that I've missed quite a few aspects of Menton itself, and I'd like to find a memento to take home with me."

"I think I'll go for a long walk round the coast as far as I can. I want to do some hard thinking."

"Hard thinking?" queried Hester. "Oh, I suppose you've an article in mind. The journalist coming to the fore."

"Well, if it's as good as the one about the Sussex Downs, it will be time well spent," said Nick, saving Josephine the trouble of replying to Hester.

"Are you two coming round the town with us?" asked Hester as they reached the exit from the gardens.

"I've still got tomorrow's jaunt to plan with Darrel," said Mike.

"I'll come," said Josephine, thinking that anything was better than her own unhappy company just then.

# 16

# Hard Thinking

It was the custom of the hotel to serve breakfast in bedrooms, and the good coffee, delicious croissants and conserves, had quite converted Josephine to the French style of breakfast. She had slept badly, and telephoned for her breakfast tray early, but when she went down to the lounge afterwards, Mike and Darrel were on the point of leaving. Nick arrived on the scene at the same time as Josephine, looking impeccable, as always.

"Good climbing, you two," he said, viewing Darrel and Mike with amused eyes. "Why spend all that effort on your feet when far greater splendours are revealed to you from the Grande Corniche in the comfort of a car, though, I can't think. The benefits of physical endeavour are much exaggerated, you know. Jean and I will see much more of the mountains today than you."

"Useless trailing your coat, you idle aesthete," said Darrel good humouredly. "I'm all in favour of a restful day for Jean, though."

Darrel's dark eyes were on Nick's fair, handsome face, and seemed to Josephine to be asking a question. Nick, whose lazy manner belied his sensitivity, looked straight at Darrel as he said,

"I'll take good care of her. You know that."

"Yes, of course. Enjoy yourselves. Hullo, darling," he added as Jean joined them. "I thought you were resting a bit longer."

"Just wanted to see you off. And you forgot this," she

added, handing him a pocket camera.

"Heavens, so I did! I'm slipping badly. Might have found some hitherto undiscovered plant with no camera to record its existence."

Mike, binoculars slung over his shoulder, was evidently covering more distant aspects than the flora of the area. They made an impressive, competent-looking pair, thought Josephine, but Mike's eyes looked tired.

"Generous of his lordship to allow me an innings today," said Nick with a mischievous sparkle in his eyes after the two men had left.

"But Darrel is a generous man," replied Jean, smiling at him. "More generous than I shall be if you raise my blood pressure on those hair-pin bends."

"Madam, your every whim shall be obeyed," said Nick with a flourish. "Even to limiting me to thirty miles an hour. Would you be willing to make an early start? I have to make the most of it, you know."

"I'll be ready in ten minutes."

"Fair enough. Fruitful thinking, Jo," he added over his shoulder as he and Jean made their way to the lift.

They were old and affectionate friends, Nick and Jean. It occurred to Josephine to wonder whether it was Jean who had once tempted Nick to abandon his bachelor ways, but then she dismissed the thought. Who was she to judge when she could not even understand the feelings of the man she had known for most of her life? Incapable of understanding, he had said.

There was more cloud about that day and a cool breeze met her as she reached the promenade and set off briskly, hoping that the exercise would stimulate her brain and do something to make her heart feel less like a cold, hard little stone inside her.

169

Painfully, she went back over the past, step by step, putting herself in Mike's shoes in an endeavour to understand. And little by little, she began to see where she had been blind, why it had gone so wrong during these past months. She realised how outrageous it must have seemed to him when she had tried to force herself into his flat that night to ask him to be friendly so that all could be smooth and easy in the circle of their mutual friends. To ask him that when at that time he could only believe that she had instigated an ugly scandal that had driven him away from Elmfield, made his job intolerable and adversely affected his father's life in the village. No wonder his reaction had been so violent.

And afterwards, when she had discovered the truth and told him. Where had she failed in understanding after that? And it dawned on her slowly that she had, as Mike had said, been bedevilled by a sense of guilt at the mischief caused by Conrad. She had felt to blame, had to atone. And that had somehow made a fatal constraint in her approach to Mike, a tentative extending of her hand which had, it seemed, incensed him. He was not the man for tentative approaches, she thought wryly.

At the end of the promenade, she took the footpath round Cap Martin, scarcely aware of her surroundings, just following the footpath. In this brooding fashion, she found herself, footsore and weary, on the outskirts of Monaco, where she found a café and had an omelette and a cup of coffee. She sat there a long time, for one of the happy aspects of café life in France was that nobody minded how long you lingered over no more than one cup of coffee. The man at the table next to hers had business papers spread all over the table, a cup of coffee almost lost among them, and was writing busily. He had been at it

170

when she arrived, and was still immersed when she finally left and wandered down to the harbour of Monaco. The sun had come through, and she sat on a seat, looking at the yachts moored there, and wondered what to do. Mike had come to the end of the road. That was certain. The decision had been taken. Had she any chance of reversing it? What could she do?

She remembered then Jean's words about the need for reassurance after rejection. He had asked her for some commitment. And anger had prevented her from responding. But surely he had every right to ask for it, since it had been she who had broken their engagement. And the commitment was there. What if it was too late, and he humiliated her by rejecting it? A kind of revenge. No. Mike was not that sort of a man. If he had been she would not love him. In any case, she ought to have answered his question yesterday.

But time was running out. There was little chance of their being alone together before they left for home. The concert was planned for that evening. They were leaving by the airport coach immediately after breakfast the next day, Friday. There was no more time, but she knew that what little chance there was of reversing his decision would be no chance at all once they had left Menton. He would see to that. It would be set and hardened and final.

She was tired out when she arrived back at the hotel late that afternoon, but she had decided what she must do. She rested on the bed for an hour, then bathed and dressed for the evening. The concert began at seven. The concert hall was only ten minutes' walk away. She gauged a time when Mike would have changed and be almost ready, and slipped along to his room at the end of the passage. Her heart was hammering uncomfortably as she

knocked at the door. His voice said, *"Entrez"*. He evidently thought she was the maid coming to turn down the bed.
She knocked again, for, unlike the maid, she had no key,
and he opened the door. Before he could say anything, she
had slipped in and closed the door behind her. He finished
knotting his tie while he looked at her, surprised.

"Hullo. What's up? A window jammed?"

"No. I want to talk to you and I know we have only a
few minutes."

He put on his jacket, saying,

"We've called it a day, Jo. No more. There's nothing to
be gained."

"Only five minutes. You asked two things of me
yesterday, Mike, to which I couldn't respond. I should
have done. But I was too angry. You asked me what I
wanted of you."

He looked at her steadily. It was harder even than she
had expected it to be. He was giving her no help. She drew
in a quivering breath, but spoke in a steady voice.

"I want you to take me back," she said simply. "And
you asked me to kiss you." She went to him and put her
arms round his shoulders. "I love you, Mike. I know
there's a lot I haven't understood, and I know I've hurt
you terribly in the past, without meaning to, but if it's not
too late to try to sort things out, if you still want me in
spite of everything, will you help me to understand?" And
she kissed him, tenderly, lingering, until she dropped her
head on his shoulder and said, "Is it too late?"

He held her there in silence for a moment or two, and
when he spoke his voice was oddly muffled.

"Jo, Jo, your timing always has been infernally bad."

"I know. What I want to ask as, perhaps, a last favour,
is, will you come round to the cottage on Saturday

172

morning, or afternoon if you plan to go in to the office in the morning, and try to make me understand what's gone wrong these past months? We shan't be interruped there. If it's just that you really do want to lose me because I remind you of what you'd sooner forget, then tell me now, and I'll get out of your way. You won't have to worry. I might go to London. I've no real base now. No set job. I can make a fresh start well away from your scene of action, leave you in peace. But if you think there's a chance of our coming together again. . ." Her voice trailed away.

He had released her and was studying her gravely.

"Not Elmfield, Jo. I can't stand the place now. It was the graveyard of so many illusions, it proved so malicious. I felt it like a frost when I went back for your mother's funeral. Come to my flat. I shan't be going to the office. I'm looking in tomorrow afternoon if the plane's on time. We shan't be interrupted there, either, since Hester is going on to London with Nick tomorrow," he concluded drily.

"All right. I'll be along about ten," she said, moving to the door.

"Jo."

She turned, her hand on the door.

"Yes?"

"Go on with the hard thinking, will you? Because you must be certain in your mind and heart. We can't put the clock back. What happened changed us, and it's a long time ago. You must be clear in your mind about the here and now. I can't take any more of this indeterminate battle. Five years is too long. There must be a final decision. So forget the guilt, forget about being kind, just be clear about what you feel and what you want."

"I am clear about what I feel. What I need is to get your side of the picture clearer."

"Until Saturday, then. Meanwhile, put it aside and enjoy the concert."

She gave him a wavery smile and slipped out of his room and back to her own to fetch her coat and bag, weak with relief at having gained, at least, a reprieve. But it would be a long time before the scars of the past were obliterated for Mike, she thought. His reference to Elmfield made that clear. Conrad had done his work well.

At the concert, she found herself sitting between Mike and Darrel. The emotional crisis of the last two days had left her strangely weak, and she listened to the Schubert symphony in a dream-like state, as though she had drifted off to another world. The orchestra was a famous one and she thought that she had never heard Debussy's *L'Après-Midi d'un Faune,* which followed the symphony, played with such exquisite sensitivity. But the nostalgic element in this combined with the stresses of that day proved her undoing, and she felt tears in her eyes which she could not stem. She felt them run down her cheeks, and kept very still, not wishing to reveal anything to Darrel or Mike. She could not have defined what she was weeping for. Those lost paths of summer when life seemed so much simpler? The scars Mike carried? The whole sorry muddle of their long relationship? Or perhaps just reaction from the desperate efforts of the day to salvage something from the wreck? A combination of all, most likely. She made an enormous effort to control her emotions as she sat there, rigid as a statue. The tears would dry off before the lights went up. And at that point, a firm, warm hand came down on the back of hers as it rested, inert, on her lap. Mike had made no other movement, seemingly intent on the orchestra, but the feel of that hand on hers was the most reassuring thing, she thought, that had ever happened to her.

\* \* \*

The supper party at their favourite little restaurant that night was a very lively one. They had all enjoyed their holiday, they said, felt better for it, and owed a debt to Hester for organising it. They therefore drank a toast of thanks to her, and she beamed on them happily.

"We make a good team," she said. "We must get together again. Perhaps Andalucia next winter. I know an excellent hotel in Algeciras for a base."

There was one maverick, thought Jo, not so keen on communal holidays, but he sipped his wine and met Jo's glance with an enigmatic smile, saying nothing.

But it was true, they had made a harmonious group, diverse as they were, and had largely followed their own bents. And tomorrow they would all be going their separate ways. Darrel and Jean had another day to spend in Menton, for they were catching the night train to Paris, and thence to Dieppe and across the Channel. From Heathrow, Nick was driving Hester into central London where she had appointments with her literary agent and publishers fixed for the following week, which she was spending in a London hotel. Mike was driving from Heathrow straight to Fordingham and the office, while she would drive back to the sad, lonely cottage in Elmfield.

For her, it had marked the end of an era, this holiday. A watershed. Her old life demolished with the loss of her mother, and her job, The future, a question mark. But about that future there was one enormously comforting factor. She and Mike were talking again. Communicating, as they had not done since that break just on five years ago. The meeting at Guy's had revealed only hostility and an enormous gulf between them. It had been followed by unnatural constraint, Mike standing her off, she hesitantly offering a timid hand. Now, at last, there was a meaningful dialogue between them, and for the first time since that traumatic meeting, she felt the old warmth of his affection there. But of the outcome, she was not sure, and she knew that she would need all the wisdom and love she could muster to overcome the breach of the years between.

# 17

# Commitment

On that Saturday morning, Josephine drove to Fordingham through cold, sleety rain that made her sigh for the kindly sun of the south. February, she thought, was one of the most spiteful months, when spring, which by the calendar was just round the corner, seemed an age away and it was hard to imagine any plants or trees having the temerity to put forth buds, although daffodils were showing through in the garden her mother had loved so much.

Mike's flat was warm and comfortable, however, and a delicious aroma of coffee greeted her when she went in.

"Foul day," he observed. "Thought you might like coffee to warm you up. Make yourself at home. I'll be with you in two shakes."

He took her coat and indicated the armchair in front of the electric fire, there more for effect than necessity, for the central heating was more than adequate. It was the first time she had set foot in his flat, although she was familiar with it from visits she had made when Guy and Sophie lived there. Mike had taken over a good deal of Guy's furniture, but it looked different, lacking Sophie's soft touches. Very functional and masculine, with books overflowing the bookcase and piled on top, papers on a desk by the window, and the general atmosphere of an office broken only by a radiogram housed in a very elegant Queen Anne cabinet which looked a little at odds with the rest of the room. A tribute to his great love, music, in a room that he obviously saw only as a base, an extension to his working life. She remembered with a shudder that time when she had tried to come in and talk to him, and the bitter exchanges outside the door. Keep away from me, Josephine, he had said savagely. And she felt a little daunted now at the prospect of trying to cross such acres of scarred battleground.

"Your twenty-fifth birthday," he said, when he came back and deposited the tray on the desk, pushing aside some papers. "Many happy returns of the day."

"You remembered?"

"I could hardly not," he said drily. "I've known you ever since the days when you wore a gym tunic, and on several occasions, seem to remember buying you a birthday present."

"Sorry. Silly remark. In fact, I'd forgotten it myself until a few birthday cards arrived this morning. I'd lost track of the date, with other things on my mind," she concluded, taking the cup of coffee from him.

After a few minutes of unnerving silence, during which she realised that again he was not going to help her, that he was going to force her into the open, she said jerkily,

"All those years between. Are they too many and too bitter to cross, Mike? I hope not."

"It's the here and now we have to face. What is between the two persons we've become that has to be settled."

"But we have to track back to understand each other now. Not to the ugliness Conrad created. That damage was done, and can't be undone. I tried to undo it, but I think the damage was too deep and long-standing. But it wasn't my fault. Have you really ever fully believed that?"

"Ninety per cent, yes. But your attitude, things you let drop to Conrad, must have put the idea into his head."

"No. I never once discussed you with him, but he did see us quarrelling that day when he opened his garden for charity. And when he saw my engagement ring was missing and asked me if our engagement was off, I just said that it hadn't worked out. They were the only two occasions he could have drawn on."

"Well, he made good use of them. Perhaps he thought you looked ill-used," said Mike drily.

"I probably didn't look my usual bonny self after the warfare that had been going on between us ever since I joined Conrad," she said bitingly, stung by his scepticism.

He gave her a wry smile then, and said,

"Sorry. Just hearing that man's name brings my fists up. I'd have like to have chucked him into his own garden pool that day, and subsequently I'd have liked to do far worse. I'd have taken him to court for libel if I'd been thick-skinned enough to have my love affair discussed in juicy detail by the press."

"Mike, if you can't believe that nothing I did or said could possibly have led Conrad to believe what he pretended to believe, that he did it purely out of self-interest because my services were of value to him, I'm never going to be able to wipe out that bitterness. It will always come between us."

"That aside, the record isn't very good, is it? The fact remains that the job meant more to you than I did. You made that plain from the moment you joined him. Not just the work, but the social side. I hardly saw you all those months. You gave yourself entirely into his service. Fair enough. You preferred the job to me. Your right. The point is, I see no reason why you should have changed your mind. I'm the same man. And I've seen no signs during these last months that you have changed your mind about where I come in your priorities."

"I thought I'd made that clear the other night."

"No, dear. I think it was kindness prompting you again. You'd seen how hurt I was, you still suffer from a sense of guilt because of what Conrad did, and I know you're fond enough of me to have been very distressed about that. But kindness isn't enough, and, indeed, is really no kindness to me, Jo. If it can't be all, it's better to be nothing and let me forget. I think it's only affection you have for me, bless you. That's why I asked you to do some hard thinking."

"It was affection when I was twenty, Mike. It's more than that now. But even then, after that last row when you were very brutal, you know, I still half-hoped that we could patch it up. I was amazed when I found that you and your father had just disappeared from the scene, leaving no addresses."

"And what were you half-hoping for? A happy little friendship for your very scarce moments of leisure? That was never on, Jo. That's where you are completely unrealistic. But I suppose that's what you had in mind, wasn't it? Be honest."

"Yes. But I was only twenty, Mike. I was fond of you. Our friendship meant a lot. But I wasn't in love with you then. I'd thought I was when we got engaged. But, well I suppose I was immature. I'd always been drawn to the literary scene, Conrad was a famous man of great charm, I met other literary figures, travelled a lot, had a wonderful time after the quiet sheltered life I'd led before. And I learned a lot about a craft I cared for. It was in a way an education. Surely, it was an understandable choice at that stage of my life. I wasn't ready for love and marriage in the fully committed way that you were. I was too young, Mike."

180

"It was a very understandable choice, my dear, and I'd be impossibly vain to think otherwise: Granted, too, that the ugliness that followed was not of your making. But was it realistic to think that I, who was fully committed and had been for years, would want to be reminded of a loss I'd never ceased to feel by some patched up lukewarm friendship to spare embarrassment all round? To see you again was the last thing I wanted. If I wasn't to have my whole life soured by frustration, I had to forget you. And then you turned up again, just when the scars had ceased to throb, and started probing at them again. But you didn't understand, did you? I loved you so much. And I lost you. And you've never understood what that feels like because you've never loved in that way."

"Until now," she said quietly. "I had to put matters right about the Conrad part. You'll grant that?"

"Yes. I appreciated that. But in a way it made matters worse. Before, I could tell myself that I was well rid of someone who could be so malicious, who could have betrayed a long-standing friendship so callously. But afterwards, when I learned that it wasn't your doing, I was left with the old deep loss."

"Which you seemed to have no desire to repair. When I left Conrad, didn't it seem to you then that I'd made a choice, a different choice?"

"Not altogether. Your honesty was shocked by his dishonesty. You'd lost your respect and admiration for him. As a person of integrity, it was not altogether surprising that you didn't want to go on working for him."

"But you were, I think, a little surprised."

"Glad that my own belief in your integrity was confirmed."

"But since then. You've been so distant. All right. You

181

didn't want a surface friendship. It would leave you frustrated. Did you have to avoid all contact so deliberately? Even to the point of rudeness? Not even have a dance with me at a Christmas party?"

"That has stuck in you, hasn't it? My dear, I couldn't move an inch towards you unless I was certain that you loved me and would marry me. There was I, trying not to slip down that hopeless path of loving you to the same dismal end that I'd experienced before, maddened by your guilty edging up and apologetic overtures of friendship."

"Well, what should I have done?" demanded Jo, driven into a corner by his legal mind.

"You know," he said quietly.

"What encouragement did I have?"

"Could you expect it? I saw no signs of any real change of heart."

"Then why did you join the holiday party if you wanted to keep away from me?"

"Two reasons seemed to offer a faint glimmering of hope. When I collected those papers you'd looked out for my father, I saw two photographs on the bookcase beside your bed. One of your parents in the garden, the other of me leaning on the stile up on the downs. That was the day I asked you to marry me. Remember?"

"Yes."

"I thought that perhaps if you wanted that by your bed, if you'd kept it all that time... And then I read your article. 'Remembered Paths of Summer.' And it seemed to me that behind it ran a deep longing for those old paths. So I thought I'd make a last effort to find out what remained in your heart for me. Only to find you flitting around with Nick and very elusive as far as I was concerned."

"It was expecting rather much after your brush-off at Christmas."

"As you pointed out to me with some vehemence. And that's when I gave up. I realised that the heart of the matter had quite passed you by."

"Yes. I worked that out for myself on the day I did my hard thinking. I'm sorry, Mike. I was playing about with the surface irritations. The knock to my petty little pride. You never were a man to pay much attention to the trivialities. But . . . it was hard when I didn't know whether you still loved me."

"You should have known. Would I have been so savage when we met again if I no longer cared? If I'd got over it, I'd have found it easy to be pleasant and friendly again, the past over and done with. But I can't compromise, Jo. Not my nature, and I can't help it. If my blood was as cool as Nick's, I could have compromised. But when you threw me over, it was like having half of me amputated, and it never really stopped feeling like that. Work was the only palliative."

"No other woman?"

He looked at her thoughtfully.

"No. I guess Hester's been talking about Penny. Penelope Rockdale. Right?"

"Yes. I saw a photograph of the two of you at a reception."

"She was a client of the firm I worked for in London. Was having some bother over a contract with a theatrical impresario. I dealt with the case and we became good friends afterwards. It was the first year after our break, and things were very black. Penny was going through a bad time, too. Her husband had died in a car accident. We answered a need in each other for help and distraction. It was never more than friendship. A warm friendship. Still

183

is. We don't see much of each other, but we can always pick up where we left off. She's playing in New York just now. You would like her. A warm, generous woman. I'm in her debt for helping me through those early months."

"I admire her acting. I'd like to meet her."

"And you? In that busy social life you led?"

"Nobody got really near. Perhaps Conrad saw to that. I don't know. But I think I was, in my subconscious, booked all the time. I kept telling myself that I'd made the right decision, and I'd be less than honest to say that I didn't enjoy those years with Conrad. My university years, in a way. But I've left them now, Mike. I know you think I was being childish about the Christmas brush-off, and so I was up to a point, but that night, I realised for the first time that I was truly in love with you, and I longed for you to take me in your arms, and it hurt. Surely now we can come together again, a little wiser, and find happiness together."

He came to her then and drew her to her feet. Holding her by the shoulders, he studied her face gravely.

"Are you sure, Jo? Quite, quite sure. Because I really couldn't go all through that again."

"I'm quite, quite sure, Mike. I only want you to give me the chance to prove it."

He smiled then, and some of the tiredness seemed to leave his face.

"Well, you can start right away," he said, and kissed her trembling mouth.

In that long kiss, the past fell away, a full commitment was made, and a beacon lit for both of them that Josephine knew would warm all their lives and never go out.

\*     \*     \*

The clock striking twelve caused Mike to lift his head and stay his roving hand.

"I've quite forgotten that I've a birthday present for you. And if I'm to curb the lusty urges of years of frustration and not risk shocking that romantic mind of yours, I'd better fetch it."

"I'm not easily shocked," she said demurely, "but I love a surprise. I didn't think that until now you were in a present-giving mood."

He pulled her ear and set her on her feet.

"I could give you the sun and the moon and the stars at the moment, even though you've been my torment for so many years. But you'll have to settle for this," he said, fetching a parcel from the bookcase.

When she opened the parcel, she found herself looking into the solemn little face of Miss Bowles with her dog.

"Oh Mike! She's been haunting me. I love her." She put Miss Bowles down gently and took Mike's face between her hands. "Thank you, my love," she said and kissed him.

"I took rather a liking to her myself. The same colour hair and eyes as yours. I always had a weakness for russety girls."

"So that's why you were so late for the airport coach yesterday and Hester was getting all anxious."

"The shopkeeper would insist on wrapping it so carefully. I feel little Miss Bowles marks a vital turning point in our lives. I shall always look on her with affection. Now, to come back to mundane matters. Are we going to have any lunch today, and if so, where? Feel like celebrating anywhere special?"

Josephine looked out of the window. The rain was still falling in steel rods from a leaden sky.

"Do you have any food here?"

"Only eggs and bread and cheese. I usually eat out."

"It feels cosy here. Could you make do with an omelette and cheese?"

"Here with a loaf of bread beneath the bough,
A flask of wine, a book of verse - and thou
Beside me singing in the wilderness -
And wilderness is Paradise enow,"

declaimed Mike with panache, before adding more soberly, "You see what a besotted state I'm in to quote verse. I leave that to literary souls like you and Nick, and prefer to stick to plain speech myself."

"Sometimes poets can express what you feel so much better."

"True. I can find a bottle of wine, and some fruit. I share your wish for privacy above all at this precise moment of time. I still can't believe it, you know," he said, serious now. "After all these years, to have you back."

"I'll convince you in time. Let's raid the kitchen. I feel very empty, having eaten no breakfast this morning because of the ordeal that confronted me."

"Was it such an ordeal?"

She lifted her eyes to his.

"I was so afraid I couldn't bridge those years between, and convince you. I still think it's going to take a long time fully to wipe out those years, but if we've learned something from them, and I think we have, perhaps that's something gained."

He nodded, then said quietly,

"How soon will you marry me, Jo? That will be the greatest reassurance of all."

186

"As quickly as arrangements can be made."

His expression then confirmed how much he had needed that reassurance. He would need it for a long time, she thought.

"Special licence? The flat will be a home until we can find a house."

"Special licence. And this will be a lovely home. Anywhere will be lovely that we share."

He took her in his arms and held her head against his shoulder.

"I love you, Jo. Don't know why it is, but I've never been able to put you out of my heart. Not even when I was hating you, which is only the other side of the same coin. I've only got to see you walk across a room, and my bones melt. I love your honest mind and your warm heart and the way you hold your head and the way you laugh with your eyes. And you don't know how hard I've tried to dismiss you."

"I did notice some of those efforts. I'll make up for it all, Mike. I promise."

"You only have to be yourself, and love me," he said simply.

\*    \*    \*

Over lunch, Mike became practical.

"Your cottage? You said you were putting it up for sale."

"Yes. You wouldn't want it for us?"

"No. Not Elmfield. You wouldn't want it, either, would you?"

"No. It would never seem ours. But it should fetch a fair price. Go a good way towards buying a house for us. You don't see this flat as a permanent answer, I gather."

"Never. We're not flat people at heart, you and I. Value privacy too much. Agreed?"

"Yes. Where would you like to live?"

"Anywhere within reasonable motoring distance of Fordingham. I know you love the downs. The choice shall be yours, of course. But not near Elmfield, Jo. No reminders of that. And, being a male chauvinist, I buy the house," he said affably as he refilled her glass of wine.

She gave him a measuring look which brought a little smile to his lips.

"Fifty-fifty?" she suggested.

"This flat should sell easily. May need a small mortgage. Depends what you set your heart on. But I'm old-fashioned enough to take it for granted that a man provides a home for his wife. You can take over the furnishing, if you want to have a stake. Don't know how much you'll want to keep from your old home. Nothing much here, probably, except my radiogram."

They went on discussing ways and means until the wine induced a decidedly unbusinesslike mood in Josephine, who started to chuckle over her coffee, feeling weak with relief and happiness and love for the dark face opposite her.

"You're not tight on two glasses of wine, are you?" demanded Mike. "Share the joke."

"I'm just visualising Hester's reaction to the news. She does so pride herself on her intuition and penetrating assessment of other people, and has been a little bothered by our inability to appreciate each other. We seem to have missed out on that fraternal feeling exising between the rest of her circle."

"I'm blessed if I'm going to wear my heart on my sleeve

just so that Hester can assess it and use it in one of her books. I've sometimes wondered whether she keeps files on us for future reference. I shall enjoy stringing dear Hester along."

"I like her. She has a very keen intelligence. You won't find it easy to string her along."

"Leave it to me. Let's clear this off, and I'll make some more coffee. Otherwise, you e going to fall asleep on me. Wine has that effect on some people."

The table cleared, Josephine sat in the armchair and waited for him to bring the coffee. But the cumulative effect of the emotional storms of the past days, sleepless hours at night, ecstatic relief and more wine than she was used to, was too much for her, and when Mike came in, she was fast asleep. He watched her while he drank his own cup of coffee, then he gently lifted her out of the chair and sat down with her in his lap. She stirred and smiled bemusedly up at him. He kissed her lightly and she snuggled down against him and fell asleep again, while Mike held her in his arms and looked to the transformed future.

# 18

# *Together Again*

Josephine wished only for a very quiet wedding, and Mike, allergic to publicity, was only too happy to agree. In the end, they kept it a secret from all but Guy and Sophie. Mike could only manage a bare week for their honeymoon, which they spent in the Scilly Islands, where bright sunshine took the chill off the fresh breezes, and daffodils that had missed the market bloomed in profusion in the fields. In their element on the sea, they spent a lot of time on the inter-island launches, and came back to Penzance tanned and brimming with vitality.

On the drive home, they stopped to visit Mike's father and aunt. Dr. Wexford greeted them with a gruffness which failed to hide his emotion.

"Mike, you young devil, not letting me know until after the event. Now your aunt will be denied the pleasure of getting out her wedding hat. She dearly loves a wedding, as you know."

"Well, in view of the recent death of Jo's mother, my dislike of publicity and the long delay since our engagement," said Mike, his lips twitching, "we thought you would excuse the fact that we simply couldn't wait to give notice of it. We were sure you would approve."

"Nothing could have made me happier. Bless you both. Jo, my dear... My dear...." He was unable to continue, and simply took her in his arms and hugged her, while Aunt Muriel with tears in her eyes embraced Mike.

But the blunt doctor, not given to emotional displays,

soon recovered and ushered them in to lunch. Afterwards Josephine left Mike and his father alone while she went round the garden with Aunt Muriel, a lengthy process for Aunt Muriel loved her plants. She had a few minutes alone with her father-in-law while Mike was fiddling with the car, which was not behaving quite up to his exacting standards.

"It's wonderful to see you both looking so well and happy, Jo. And to see the difference in Mike. I never thought you'd be able to do it. He'd changed, and hardened so much."

"But he still loved me. Miraculously, that had survived. I'll do my best to make up for it all. I love him dearly."

"And that is all he wants. He's not an easy man to handle," he added sharply. "Going to be up to it? Not be dominated?"

"I always have been up to it. I've never been daunted or the least bit afraid of Mike, you know. Not even when we were young. That volcanic element is well under control now, but it never did worry me. I rather liked it. A challenge. Never boring. And no nasty taste lingering after the blow-ups. Not until the final blow-up. And the nasty taste of that is dwindling far more quickly than I expected."

"That's obvious. Yes, I guess you understand him, and have your own way of holding your ground. Well, Mike," he added, turning as his son came up. "Fixed it to your satisfaction?"

"More or less. Wants a thorough overhaul. It'll get us home all right, I guess. What prescriptions has he been doling out to you, Jo? I know that look of his, directed at patients in need of firm guidance."

"You two are obviously not in need of anything that

191

you're not getting just now. I was just warning Jo not to be too soft with you."

"Soft? You don't know how much she's changed. Once a dear little turtle dove. Now. . ." He shook his head sadly. "A much tougher proposition."

"A toughness you enjoy, no doubt."

"Bear with us. A rush of nonsense to the head has beset us for the past few weks. We'll become sane again in due course, I guess. Now we must be off. A long way to go."

"You'll not do it in one hop?"

"Probably stop the night in Winchester if Jo's tired. Take care of yourselves. We'll come down for a weekend before long."

Dr. Wexford put a hand on his son's shoulder for a moment, their eyes meeting.

"Life's come good for you, Mike."

"Very good."

The old man squeezed his shoulder and walked out with them to the car. No need to tell Mike to cherish their happiness, rare in this world, for his son had won it too hardly not to value it. Jo had a lot of her father in her, he thought. A dear girl. It was a long time since he had felt so happy. And for once, he was not irritated by Muriel's sentimental gush as she took his arm, saying brightly,

"Wasn't it splendid to see those two happy young people? So much in love. And dear Mike so rejuvenated. They were always meant for each other. I do declare I feel quite rejuvenated myself, what with those two dear children, and the crocuses in bloom, and the almond tree. All so romantic, and the dark days of winter over."

"Quite so, my dear," he said, patting her hand, and reflecting that his sister, who had never been loved by a man, and had little idea, he sometimes thought, of what it was all about, had retained an innocent delight in romance that any modern teenager would have scorned, and had never been soured by envy or neglect. On any other day, he would have said that only inexperience could have preserved such romantic illusions, but scepticism was out of place on that day, and he added, "Quite so. Love is a very warming thing to behold, and has great therapeutic qualities."

*   *   *

Mike's michievous plan to put Hester out of countenance was helped by circumstances which he could not have arranged more favourably if he had thought about it for weeks.

Hester had followed her stay in London with two weeks in Scotland researching a background for her next novel, so that by the time she was back in her flat, Mike and Josephine had returned from their honeymoon and had been living in the flat together for a week. It was on the Sunday morning when Mike was making early tea for the two of them and glancing at the *Sunday Times* that a knock at his door revealed Hester.

"Oh, you are up, Mike. Sorry to bother you so early, but I'm right out of coffee, and can't face the day without it. Got back too late last night to do anything about it."

Mike, reacting rapidly, appeared to hesitate a moment, then said hurriedly,

"Sure. Sure, Hester. Come in. I'll raid the kitchen. Only coffee bags. Those do you?"

"Fine. That's a dashing line in boudoir wear," she added, eyeing the gold unicorns prancing over the maroon background of Mike's dressing gown topping blue pyjamas.

"No good asking you if you're tempted, since you're obviously in a very business-like mood, and so early in the morning!" said Mike, shaking his head at Hester's trim blouse and skirt.

"Want to get to work straight away. Had a good idea for a plot yesterday. Worked it out in the train. Want to get it down while it's fresh in my mind."

"Won't be a sec, then," replied Mike, surreptitiously pushing the tray with its two cups to one side, gleefully aware that Hester's glance had just fallen on them. "Like to read the headlines?" he added, handing her the *Sunday Times*.

Once out of sight, he slid quickly along to the bedroom, gave Jo her instructions, returned to the kitchen and fished about for the coffee bags. He knew from the slightly embarrassed expression on Hester's face that the implication of the two cups on the tray had not passed her by.

"Half a dozen see you through?" he asked casually, handing the coffee bags over.

"Fine. Thanks a lot. Sorry for barging in at such an hour."

"Don't mention it." He hurried to the door, his quick ear catching a rustling sound, and opened it. "My pleasure," he said, then, as Hester made to go, Jo's head came round the sitting-room door, saying,

"Mike, darling, how much longer are you going to be with that tea? I'm. . ." She stopped dead as she saw Hester. There was a pregnant silence. Then Jo said a little weakly, "Oh, hullo, Hester. Didn't know you were back," and hovered there, hastily buttoning up a frilly pink dressing-gown to hide the somewhat diaphanous night-dress beneath.

"Well, a fair cop," said Mike with what was obviously assumed heartiness. "Hester's out of coffee. Good thing you're a women's-libber, Hester."

Across Hester's face flitted amazement, shock, embarrassment, incredulity. Mike had to turn away and cough to hide his amusement, but Jo stood there, a picture of indeterminate confusion.

"Well, I *have* come at an awkward time," said Hester, pulling herself together. "Funny. I was sure you two were poles apart." She looked at Josephine now as though at some extraordinary phenomenon, then, flushing, she added hurriedly, "Sorry, Mike. I'll phone next time. And thanks for the coffee," and bolted.

Mike closed the door behind her and striding across the room to his wife, hugged her joyfully.

"Darling, you were superb. The picture of guilty confusion. If you weren't such a good writer, I'd suggest you took up acting."

"A bit naughty of us."

"Nonsense. No lies were uttered. I shall carry with me to the grave the joyous picture of Hester's face trying to reconcile her women's-lib principles with her instinctive shock when her friends put them into practice. Oh, happy day! What's the betting that Hester's back-tracking to see what signs she overlooked?"

"When are we going to reveal all?"

"Not until we have to," he said, still laughing and unrepentant.

"If the kettle's on, it's probably boiling its head off by now."

"I turned it off. You know, you look very, very cuddly

in that outfit. Are your thoughts really set on tea, or could it wait a little?"

She shook her finger at him, her eyes lowered, her voice grave.

"Hester has put lascivious thoughts into your mind, Mike."

He tilted her chin and met her dancing eyes.

"Are you preferring tea to my loving attentions?"

"Of course," she said, and as he lifted an admonishing hand, broke away and scuttled back to bed, Mike on her heels.

* * *

Hester kept away from the flat for the following week, until on the Saturday afternoon she knocked at the door with some photographs of their holiday. Her manner was extremely crisp.

"Thought you might like to see these," she said to Mike, who opened the door. She made no effort to come in until he made a point of inviting her, saying cheerfully,

"Nothing to embarrass you this time, Hester. Come in and let's have a look at them together."

Josephine was sitting at a table littered with estate agents' forms, and looked up with a smile as Hester came in.

"How's the plot?"

"A bit sticky. The best ones are of Monaco," she said, obviously determined to keep to impersonal topics, then, as Josephine collected up the forms to make room on the table, she caught sight of a glinting ring. She pounced, pinning Josephine's left hand to the table. There, un-

196

deniably, was a plain wedding ring and an engagement ring of diamonds surrounding a ruby heart.

"Jo!" she exclaimed, then turned to Mike. Their expressions were enough. "You *wicked* people!" she exclaimed, more outraged than ever before. "You sly, secretive, wicked people."

"You must forgive us, Hester. We couldn't resist the temptation," said Josephine, her eyes laughing.

"Never! I'll never forgive such deception. When?"

"Three weeks ago," said Mike.

"A bit impulsive, wasn't it?" asked Hester, now seemingly dazed.

"Hardly. We were engaged five years ago."

Hester ran her hands through her hair, making it stand out like a scarecrow, and said,

"All right. I'll buy it. I thought you were my close friends, and now find I know nothing about you. Did you have to be so secretive?"

Josephine sensed some hurt behind Hester's words, and said gently,

"Our history goes back a long time before we knew you, Hester. It's a complex and painful one we don't care to talk about. We came together again and wiped out the past only on the day after we got back from Menton. We'd lost so many years, we didn't want to waste any more time. You were away. Nobody knew except Guy and Sophie, but we're going to throw a party in two weeks' time and ask you all to forgive us. I'm sorry we couldn't resist that act, but when you burst in on us that morning, it was so beautifully set up for us."

"I'd say. Well, stop looking so complacent, Mike, although I admit that you've every reason to be. Another good, talented girl lost. But I love you both, and I'll forgive you. How could I have been so obtuse, though? I never caught a hint. Usually, you can sense these sort of things. At least, I can. Am I slipping, or are you two unusually cunning? I'd have been less surprised if it had been Nick. You two seemed to keep a wary distance from each other like cat and dog."

"Passions are likened best to floods and streams;
The shallow murmur, but the deep are dumb,"

quoted Mike with an extravagant gesture, drawing a look of amazement from his wife and Hester.

"Darling, you really are getting as good as Nick at the apt quotation," said Josephine.

"I came across that only yesterday when I was glancing through one of your anthologies," he said modestly.

"And who was responsible for it?" asked Hester.

"That doughty hero, Sir Philip Sydney."

"Well," said Hester, shaking her head, "you've certainly worked wonders with Mike in a short time, Jo. I'm accustomed to finding him surrounded by legal papers, frowning and preoccupied with dark thoughts, and here he is positively sparkling and quoting romantic poetry to me. And to think of the times I've remarked on his bitterness and wondered, in your presence, my girl, who the female was who had caused the frost-bite, and you listened, all mum and innocent."

"Well, people aren't peeled so easily, Hester, even by writers as skilful as you," said Mike. "The frosty season is over now, though. What about coming out to dinner with us this evening, to show you forgive us?"

"Reparation accepted. You know, you two have quite messed up my work this week. Couldn't get you out of my

198

mind when I should have been immersed in my plot."

"Really? Surely your liberated outlook should have taken that little episode in your stride, and approved the experiment," said Mike blandly.

"I'm not being drawn on that reprehensible episode any more. You're both very happy and sure about it, that's plain, so I'm happy, too. And since those are details about houses for sale, I suppose you're thinking of deserting me," concluded Hester plaintively.

"Shan't be going far. Mike has to be within reasonable reach of Fordingham," said Josephine.

"It's always the same. As soon as I get someone I like installed in this flat, he gets a girl and ups and goes. Guy was the same. Have you found what you want yet?"

"One hopeful. We're going to see it again tomorrow morning. At Ashbrook. Not too far away."

"Well," said Hester, sighing, "try to sell this flat to a nice settled widower, or retired headmistress, will you, Mike? I don't like all this chopping and changing. And I shall miss you, my dark, handsome chauvinist."

Mike smiled and gave her a kiss.

"I'll do my best for you. And we shall be seeing you often, we hope."

"Well, I'll leave those photographs with you and get back and try to do some work. You're a very distracting couple," she observed from the door. "Bless you both."

\*     \*     \*

The house was called Challoners. It stood on its own, about half a mile out of the village of Ashbrook, where the wooded valley flattened out between two arms of the downs. Of brick and timber, it was of modest size, with

199

small-paned bay windows on the ground floor, and deep-eaved flat windows above. It sat in a half acre plot of overgrown garden, and had a deep, wide porch, over and around which was a tangle of roses and honeysuckle. Pleasing but unremarkable outside, they had found many appealing features inside, including fine old oak doors in arched doorways to all the rooms, unusual and handsome wrought-iron wall brackets, and in the sitting-room a wide, deepset hearth and fireplace which would comfortably house the largest log fire imaginable. The house was the right size for them, and its seclusion was safe, for the woods at the back were on protected land, and the fields in front were grazing land right up to the slope of the South Downs.

"It still feels good," said Josephine, who had wondered whether the first favourable impressions might dwindle on a second visit.

"Yes." Mike, who had been poking into cupboards, joined her by an upstairs window. "Seems dry enough everywhere although it's been empty for some time."

"A house that feels warm and friendly even when it's bare and empty must have a lot going for it. I'm sure the people who lived here before were happy. I feel it in the air."

Mike smiled at such foolishness and put an arm round her shoulders.

"You'd like it?"

"Yes. No doubts. The right size, the right place, within our means, and available as soon as a contract can be drawn up and signed."

"Right. As it's an executors' sale, they won't want to hang about. We'll have a survey, just to be sure of what

200

we're taking on. That garden's a fine old mess, but has possibilities, I'd say."

"Do you think it would be stealing to pick those daffodils to take back to the flat?"

"Not as we'll be paying a deposit to the agents tomorrow."

They left the daffodils in the car and walked across the field where sheep and lambs were grazing to climb the path up to the crest of the downs. With the familiar song of the larks high above them and the soft south-west wind in their faces, they swung along. This end of the downs was more folded than the downs in the Elmfield area, some twenty miles to the east of them, and a little more wooded, but the same sense of freedom, the same hint of the sea in the air, the same wide horizons, cast their spell over Josephine as of old. Rooks were building high, wheeling and calling above a beech-hanger as they passed by. The grass was shining in the clear March sunshine, and she saw a few violets blooming there. As she squared her shoulders and felt the soft breeze catch her hair, a heady exaltation seized her and she said,

"I feel uplifted. As though I'm sprouting wings."

"Please stay earth-bound. I need you."

They stopped for a rest and leaned on a gate. Puffy white clouds sailed across the blue sky like wandering sheep, and in the distance, framed by the folds of the downs, a small glittering triangle of sea was visible. What a lot had happened to her in just one month, she thought. The shattering scene with Mike in Menton, when all seemed lost. Their marriage. Honeymoon. And now Challoners. She no longer felt the same person as the one who had set out for Menton. Could no longer imagine a life without Mike there, sharing it. He had felt as though

201

half of him had been amputated when he lost her, he had said, and she understood that feeling, for she would be in like plight now without him. In loving him, she had discovered things about herself, as well as Mike, that she had never suspected. Most surprising of all, perhaps, had been the passion in her which his passion had been able to arouse, something unknown and unguessed at before. And with the full flowering of her love for him, she understood fully how inadequate her approaches to him had been after that meeting at Guy's house-warming party, comprehended the violence of his reaction. It was not a tame man she had married. Nor would she have him otherwise.

She glanced at him. He was gazing into the distance, where the sea glittered, a rare serenity on his dark face. Wherever his thoughts were, he was in a state of tranquillity which she would not break. She looked at his lean brown hand resting on the gate. Strong but sensitive, capable of being wonderfully gentle. And since they had come together again, his tenderness had been a heart-melting revelation.

She turned her gaze back to the rounded contours of the downs. They had both known and loved this landscape all their lives. The paths of summer. Remembering that sad little poem which had haunted her, seeing in it her destiny, she was inexpressibly thankful that it had not said the last word for her, that she and Mike would walk those summer paths again, and knit the strands of their lives together in that small house under these same downs.

# DENISE ROBINS

## JEZEBEL

Jezebel's reception into Samaria was hailed as one of the wonders of the world. Drenched in the exotic colours of the East, the spectacle of Ahab's bride and her triumphant progress to the Ivory Palace was never to be forgotten. Yet even then, amid the cheering voices, there were those who seemed to sense a dreadful power in Jezebel's stately bearing. Her beauty brought her praise and admiration from all who served her. But as Thamar, her half-sister had foreseen, the seeds of Jezebel's glory were later to bear a terrible fruit. For her evil and tyranny would one day earn her the title of the wickedest woman in the world.

'A brilliantly plausible re-creation – a fascinating achievement'

*She*

'Denise Robins is an expert romancer.'

*The Sunday Times*

**CORONET BOOKS**

# ELIZABETH CADELL

## DECK WITH FLOWERS

Madame Landini's memoirs promised to be sensational. Rodney, who had captured them for his publishing house, could congratulate himself on a brilliant coup. And so could his friend Oliver, Madame Landini's literary agent. But having covered her childhood as a Russian princess, her years of exile in Paris and the discovery of her phenomenal voice, the prima donna reached her first husband's death — 'man overboard' — and declared she would write no more.

Rodney suspected that there was more to her change of heart than a display of temperament. He hoped that perhaps Nicola Baird, Madame Landini's dismissed secretary, could help solve the mystery. But Nicola was beautiful as well as elusive and Rodney found himself becoming romantically entangled with her. Meanwhile Oliver, although engaged to another girl, was at last beginning to return the constant affection of Rodney's sister Angela . . .

**CORONET BOOKS**

**HERMINA BLACK**

IN THE TIME OF LILACS

When Alec Dering saw a taxi hurtle to a stop outside his father's chambers he little realised that the young girl who sprang out was to alter the course of his life. For Retta had an extraordinary story to tell. So extraordinary that in the absence of his lawyer father Alec felt compelled to offer her his protection. Even though it meant taking her to Paris while he completed business over his latest play.

In Paris the lilacs were blooming, and as the beautiful spring days went by, Retta gradually forgot the horror of her past. And she reluctantly admitted to herself that she had fallen in love with a confirmed bachelor. Alec was a sardonic man of the world, and now that he had seen her to the safety of a friend's home, he had no intention of becoming further involved.

And then, suddenly, the shadow of the man Retta feared threatened her again . . .

**CORONET BOOKS**

# DENISE ROBINS

## LAURENCE, MY LOVE

Having spent twelve years within the confines of a
Belgian convent, Vere Rowland s meeting on the journey
home with Laurence Bracknell was as pleasant as it was
unexpected. It transpired that Laurence lived within a
short distance of the Great Gatehouse, where her mother
was housekeeper to the Halbertsons. But this coincidence
led to some troublesome questions.

Before the answers to these questions were known,
there was much to be borne and much to be suffered —
but then, life is never easy when you're in love.

'Rarely has a writer of our times delved so deeply into the
secret places of a woman's heart.'

*Taylor Caldwell*

**CORONET BOOKS**

# ELIZABETH CADELL

## ROUND DOZEN

William Helder was a man living alone, a man with no financial worries and no responsibilities outside his work. He was not an adventurous person.

It was his stepmother who insisted he should find the lost flagon which was the last of a set of twelve small silver pieces presented to the family by King William and Queen Mary in 1689. Over the years several had been lost and all recovered save this last delicate and beautiful antique. The untimely death of William's father had abruptly closed the link with a dealer at Steeplewood and so William set out to reopen the connection and search once more.

He could have had little idea how his life would be changed and enriched as his quest intensified, nor how grateful he would be at the end for his stepmother's kindly interference.

**CORONET BOOKS**

# MORE ROMANCE FROM CORONET BOOKS

**IRIS BROMIGE**

☐ 22336 7 A Haunted Landscape      60p
☐ 24398 8 A Distant Song      75p

**HERMINA BLACK**

☐ 21254 3 In The Time Of Lilacs      60p
☐ 02478 X Stardust For Dreams      60p

**ELIZABETH CADELL**

☐ 19863 X Deck With Flowers      60p
☐ 23097 5 Parson's House      80p
☐ 24712 6 Round Dozen      85p

**DENISE ROBINS**

☐ 26100 5 Lucrezia      £1.25
☐ 23320 6 Jezebel      85p
☐ 12963 8 Laurence, My Love      60p

*All these books are available at your local bookshop or newsagent, or can be ordered direct from the publisher. Just tick the titles you want and fill in the form below.*

Prices and availability subject to change without notice.

---

CORONET BOOKS, P.O. Box 11, Falmouth, Cornwall.

Please send cheque or postal order, and allow the following for postage and packing:

U.K.—One book 30p, 15p for the second book plus 12p for each additional book ordered, up to a maximum of £1.29.

B.F.P.O. and EIRE—30p for the first book, 15p for the second book plus 12p per copy for the next 7 books; thereafter 6p per book.

OTHER OVERSEAS CUSTOMERS—50p for the first book plus 15p per copy for each additional book.

Name ...............................................................................

Address ...........................................................................

.........................................................................................